SO YOU LOVE TO HATE YOUR BOSS

SO YOU WANT TO BE A BILLIONAIRE BOOK 2

ELIZABETH MADDREY

Scripture quoted by permission. Quotations designated (NIV) are from THE HOLY BIBLE: NEW INTERNATIONAL VERSION®. NIV®. Copyright © 1973, 1978, 1984 by Biblica. All rights reserved worldwide.

Cover design by Indie Cover Design (Lynnette Bonner)

Published in the United States of America by Elizabeth Maddrey

www.ElizabethMaddrey.com

Publisher's Note: This novel is a work of fiction. Names, characters, places, and incidents are either products of the author's imagination or used fictitiously. All characters are fictional, and any similarity to people living or dead is purely coincidental.

1

C hristopher Ward scanned the conference room. Everyone milling around by the coffee and snacks or seated over by the table were pretty much the people he expected to see at this meeting. He hadn't, actually, anticipated his own invitation.

Wanted it?

Craved it?

Absolutely.

And still it had been a shock—a good one—when it had shown up in his email the day before New Year's Eve.

Who else was here from the Government Services Group, though?

Movement caught his eye and he watched Stephanie Collins push through the crowd by the coffee with a mug in her hands and make her way to the table.

His heart sank. Stephanie? Seriously?

Maybe the big boss's heart attack in September had affected him more than he was letting on.

Oh, sure, after Christopher had gone to Joe and complained about Stephanie, the problem had been solved. Stephanie was almost pleasant to work with now. The problem, of course, was that it should be obvious to everyone that it was all just for show. She was still the same cold-hearted "b" word underneath her gritted-teeth smiles and fluttery eyelashes.

He took a deep breath. So it was Stephanie. That was fine. He could beat her at this game and end up taking home the new title and top position. He could do that in his sleep. He already had a huge advantage, because the teams who worked in the GSG all liked him, and they were, at best, ambivalent about her. It would make it easier for him to get them to perform, and surely that was going to be a major element of success in this competition.

For now, he'd make nice.

Christopher skipped the coffee—there was better available at a number of kiosks within an easy walk from the office, and he wasn't going to settle for the industrial grade if he didn't have to—and made his way to the empty seat beside Stephanie.

"Is this seat taken?"

Stephanie glanced up. Just for an instant her face looked like she'd bitten into something sour, then it morphed into a too-bright smile. "Of course not. Good to see you, Chris."

"Christopher." He muttered it as he pulled out his chair and sat. The seats were impressively soft. Of course, this was the executive conference room, and it was pretty clear Joe Robinson, the owner and founder of the corporation, had spared no expense. Not that Joe did a lot of expense sparing—the guy believed in treating his employees well. "Can you believe this?"

"The conference room? I've been here a couple of times before."

Now it was Christopher's turn to grind his teeth together behind his grin. He took a deep breath—gosh, she shouldn't smell good. That wasn't fair at all. "No. The restructuring. The contest. Whatever all this is."

"Oh." She shook her head, her smile slipping slightly. "Not really. It's not what I'd do, but then again, I've never been in that situation before. Maybe it makes sense once you have."

Christopher didn't quite catch the snort of disbelief.

Stephanie's smile warmed for a moment. She shrugged. "Anyway, if Joe wants to break up the company so he has more free time, then I'm going to do my best to make sure that our clients get the best out of it."

Clever girl. There was nothing to say in response to that. Christopher couldn't talk about fighting to make sure he ended up in charge. That would make it about him. And, as much as he didn't want to admit it, it wasn't. Or not all of it. The customer was definitely the most important part of anything they did in the GSG. They had contracts supporting the Pentagon and troops who were deployed around the world. "Absolutely."

"Hey, bro."

Christopher glanced over as his younger sister, Jessica, slid into the seat beside him. "Jess. You're here?"

Jessica waggled her eyebrows. "Best of the best, you know it. Ry's getting coffee."

Christopher nodded. His best friend, Ryan, made sense. He was one of the top-tier managers already in the cyber security division of the company. But his sister? Wasn't she more of a grunt? What was Joe doing? "Hey, Ryan."

Ryan raised his coffee cup in greeting before sitting on the other side of Jessica.

Christopher glanced back at Stephanie. She was watching them with interest. Ugh. He should probably make introductions. He cleared his throat. "Stephanie, have you met my sister? Or Ryan Foster? They're both in cyber."

"Hi. Jessica Ward. I'd prefer not to be known as Christopher's sister whenever possible." Jessica held out her hand with a friendly grin.

Stephanie laughed and shook it. "Stephanie Collins."

Ryan leaned forward. "I think I consulted on a proposal effort you were running a couple of months ago."

"Right. Thanks for that. We won. You definitely helped." Stephanie's forehead wrinkled lightly. "I think we actually shuttled some of the work over to cyber."

Ryan's eyebrows rose. "Did you? I'll have to investigate. I'd be interested in getting in on that. It was a fascinating network security problem. It'd be fun to solve."

"I'll take a look when I'm back in my office and get in touch." Stephanie jotted a note on the pad in front of her.

"Appreciate it." Ryan sipped his coffee. He glanced at Christopher and started to speak, but stopped when Joe strode into the room.

"If you'd all find a seat, we can get started." Joe grinned as he took the chair at the head of the conference table and settled in it. The few stragglers who'd been by the coffee all made their way to the table. "Good. Great. Thanks, everyone, for making time in your day to attend this meeting."

Christopher chuckled. He wasn't the only one. Would anyone have declined the offer to possibly take over an arm of the multi-billion dollar company Joe had founded? Unlikely. It was almost guaranteed that the people in those positions would, themselves, become millionaires. Maybe more than that. Christopher wasn't only in it for the money, but he wasn't going to say no, either.

He could do a lot of good—make a big difference in the world—with a bigger disposable income. He glanced around the table and counted. Nine plus Joe? Shouldn't there be ten, if there was going to be a contest for each of the five arms?

He shook his head to clear it and focused back on Joe.

"Tyler will hand out packets of information when we're finished here. They'll have all the details, and if you have any questions, Tyler's going to be your point man. I'm also available, of course, but my schedule is a little busier than Ty's, so I won't always be able to get back to you quickly. If it's urgent, reach out to Tyler first. If he thinks the situation needs me, he knows how to get a hold of me at all times."

Christopher nodded. Tyler Shaw had been Joe's right-hand man since Christopher joined the company. It made sense that he'd be up to his elbows in all of this. And maybe as a reward he got to choose one of the branches to head up? It didn't seem fair that he wouldn't have to compete, but whatever. It wasn't Christopher's decision.

Joe steepled his fingers and leaned back in his chair. "You were each chosen because of your skills, but also because of the areas where your skills are lacking. If you look around, you should see one other person from your arm of the company here today. They possess the skills you lack. One of the biggest measurements of success is going to be how the two of you work together to achieve success."

Welp. He was sunk.

He stealthily glanced at Stephanie. Both of them were sunk.

Compete against one another? Sure, they could absolutely do that. But work together? They'd already proven that was an uphill battle.

"... think of more as a collaboration than a competition."

Oh, great. He'd missed some of what Joe was saying. *Focus, Christopher.*

Stephanie was smirking.

"We'll have a check-in meeting the first Monday of each month. You'll get calendar invites from my admin for those soon. Barring major catastrophe, both of you need to be in attendance at those meetings. Beyond that? Expect to be watched. Expect Tyler or me to stop by with questions here and there. I can't give you a checklist that will automatically result in success. It's not that quantifiable. I know that frustrates . . . probably all of you." Joe laughed. "But you wouldn't have been chosen if you weren't capable. That's not the question."

"What is the question then, sir?"

Joe smiled. "Of all the people at the table, Melanie, you're the most likely to understand. For those of you who don't know Melanie, she's one of the head writers for our video game division. The question I'm looking to answer isn't who's competent to run the business. It's who brings the right chemistry to the team. I'm looking for synergy, more than anything."

SYNERGY? Stephanie managed not to snicker out loud, but it was close. She glanced over at Chris—she made herself stop and mentally amend it to Christopher—and pressed her lips together. This was going to be annoying. He was listening to Joe intently—like the man was imparting the very words of God or something. She'd had soldiers like that. They were the ones who ended up dying young most of the time because they were too busy following orders to employ their brains. Orders didn't always make sense. Anyone who followed blindly was bound to get burned for it eventually.

She caught herself before she rubbed her left arm.

"Any other questions?" Joe made eye contact with everyone sitting at the table. Even the mousy girl from social media—what was her name? She defined "flying under the radar," whatever it was. How had she even ended up in this conference room? "I'll take the silence as 'no,' but if that changes, you know how to get a hold of Tyler or me. Don't plan any vacations for the next six months—not if you're expecting to succeed. There's more to life than work, but at the same time, I expect the people who take over to understand that balance doesn't always look like nine to five, Monday through Friday. Work hard when it's needed, and play when you're finished."

Stephanie nodded, watching as Joe stood. Vacation wasn't a priority for her. She'd seen enough of the world in the Army. Time off was better spent learning something or working out. Maybe both. Anything that kept her mind too busy to sink back into nightmares.

"Your first assignment, due in two weeks, is a five-year plan for your company. Just one." Joe pointed a finger at each of the pairs. "I'm serious about the collaboration thing. If you need any historical data to help inform your choices for the future, let me or Tyler know, and we'll make it available to you, if it isn't already. Let's get to work."

Joe nodded to Tyler before he strode from the room.

Tyler gestured to a pile of folders. "I have information packets. Make sure you take the one with your name on it, as some of the data is personalized for your specific situation. The first page has my cell number as well as other contact details. Reach out when you need me, but keep in mind I'm working on the same assignments for the business applications arm."

"You don't have a competitor." Stephanie pressed her lips together as soon as the words finished spewing out. Tone. She needed to control her tone *before* it got away from her.

Tyler sent her a long, cool look. "No. I don't. It's mine unless I screw up. There are reasons behind that decision, but I'm reasonably sure if Joe felt you needed to know what they were, he'd tell you."

Heat washed over her—a combination of shame and anger. Words bubbled in her throat, desperate to escape. Stephanie clenched her hands into fists under the table and retrained her response to a sharp nod.

"Anyone else?" Tyler's gaze flicked from person to person at the table.

Stephanie stared straight ahead, unseeing. She was sure Tyler would be reporting that little outburst to Joe, and it'd be just another black mark on her record. At least he'd managed to overlook the unfair bias against her that came with being an outspoken, intelligent woman and put her on the list to be considered.

She was the better person for the job. She knew that deep in her bones.

But she was also her own worst enemy.

"Okay. Grab your folder on your way out. Joe gave you two weeks for the five-year plan. I want to see drafts in one. If you're completely off base, you're better off knowing while you still have time to fix it." Tyler offered a tight smile before he left the room.

"Nice going." Christopher muttered in her ear as he stood.

Stephanie ground her teeth. She wasn't going to rise to his bait. Not in front of everyone else. She could *feel* them watching her. Everyone always did. Oh, sure, she had a reputation as someone who exploded, who was difficult to work with, and it was probable that the whole "morale issue" had made the rounds. They probably all laughed at her when they got together after work hours.

Well, let them.

She'd see who was laughing after she won.

Stephanie stood and waited for her chance to snag the folder with her name in clear block letters across the front. Cradling it to her, she made her way to the door, not bothering to even try to stop and chat with anyone as she left. It wasn't as if they'd be interested.

In the hall, she lengthened her stride. She needed to get outside—breathe in some of the cool air and get herself back under control.

"Steph, wait!"

Fighting a groan, she stopped and turned, arms crossed.

Christopher jogged up to her, a questioning look on his features. "Are you okay?"

"Of course. Why wouldn't I be?" Silence hummed between them for a moment before he shrugged. That was good. At least he didn't push.

He cleared his throat. "Did you want to get together and divvy up the five-year plan?"

Gosh, that would be great. But it was also the fastest way to fail. "I don't think divvying it up is the way to go."

"But—"

"Look, you hate me. I get it. But Joe said to work together. I think he meant it literally. We can try it your way if you insist, but that's going to end up with us starting from scratch with only one week instead of two."

"You don't know that."

But she did. Deep in her gut, she knew. Just like she'd known a lot of things in the Army. And the times when she'd failed to listen, the consequences had always been costly. She swallowed. She was supposed to get along. Mostly that seemed to mean let other people be wrong and then not say, "I told you so." Stephanie fought a sigh. "Fine."

"Great. So maybe in an hour? I can come to your office and we can—"

"Just send me an email with the parts you want to do. I'll do the rest." If they were going to do it wrong from the get-go, she might as well avoid unnecessary meetings.

"Are there pieces you'd rather do?"

She shook her head. She hadn't specifically written a five-year business plan before, but that was what the Internet was for. Let Christopher choose his parts and she'd fill in whatever he didn't choose. "Just try to leave me something."

"What's that supposed to mean?" He crossed his arms.

"Like I said, I know you hate me. Everyone does. Big whoop. I'm good at my job and that's what matters. Joe said we're supposed to work together, which means you won't get away with trying to do it all and then asking me to rubber stamp it. First off, I won't do it. And second, Joe will know. He's cagy that way. So choose half, and let me know what's left for me."

"I wasn't going to—"

Stephanie held up her hand, sent him a scornful look, and spun on her heel. She strode down the hall while Christopher sputtered. Whatever. He was already trying to cut her out? Fine. She'd still claw her way to the top.

If the Army had taught her anything, it was how to stay alive at all costs.

2

S tephanie closed her office door and went to stand at her window. She'd taken twenty minutes to walk one of her cool-off routes. Between the cold January air and the exercise, she had herself under control. Mostly. At least the urge to run her fingers over the ridges of the keloidal scarring that consumed her left arm had abated. Thankfully, the scars evened out almost two inches above her wrist, so if she wore long sleeves, they stayed hidden.

She didn't need pity.

She didn't want it.

It was bad enough the injury had cost her a career in the Army—the only career she'd planned on having. So now she was here, in an office, making nice with a man who had to be the most annoying human God ever created.

Stephanie winced and muttered a quick prayer of apology. Christopher was made in God's image, the same as she was. But man. Why did loving people have to be so hard?

Breathe in ... two ... three ... four ...

She counted to ten as she inhaled, tapping a finger on her leg with each number. She held her breath, tapping off a five count before exhaling for a ten count. Stephanie repeated the process twice more, stopping as her heart slowed and calm settled back into place like a nicely fitting cape.

She turned and took a seat at her desk, wiggled the mouse, and logged in. Sixteen email messages. She only cared about one right now. Had Christopher gotten her the assignments she needed?

"Probably should've been the one to make the assignments. I outrank him," she muttered under her breath as she scanned for his name in her inbox, then clicked. "No, got to get along with him. Be a team player."

She eyed the breakout of work and nodded. At least it was equal. And it didn't look like he'd tried to hog all the interesting parts, either. If she had to guess, he'd ticked off every other one for himself and given her the rest.

Huh.

Stephanie typed out a quick confirmation and acknowledgement then paused, her fingers hovering over her keyboard. They really should meet and make sure when they put it all together that it was cohesive. She added the suggestion, along with a couple of options for when her calendar was clear, and clicked Send. He could say no. She wasn't going to push. But it still felt like divvying up the work this way was going to bite them both in the tail.

She glanced over her list of items for the five-year plan one more time before switching back to her inbox. She still had her regular job to do. The extra work could be done in the evenings or if she had downtime. She wasn't going to shirk her responsibility all for a chance at promotion. Hopefully, Christopher wouldn't either.

Should she remind him?

No.

That wasn't going to reflect on her either way, so she'd let him figure it out for himself. For now, it looked like she needed to go talk with Rick about his impending deadline. It wasn't something squishy he could ignore.

With a sigh, Stephanie pushed away from her desk. She tucked her phone in her pocket, locked her computer, and headed out into the sea of cubicles that formed the bulk of this floor of the building. She had one of the offices around the outer edge, one she didn't have to share. It was a huge blessing. There were times—multiple times a day—when she needed to close her door and take a minute or two.

Of course, if people weren't the way they were, maybe she wouldn't need to and she'd be able to manage in a cube, but she didn't want to put it to the test.

She slowed her pace and tapped on the metal surrounding the entrance to Rick's cube.

He glanced over his shoulder and sagged. "Stephanie. You didn't have to come over here. I told you everything in the email."

"Rick. We don't have any play in the timeline. You've got to know that." She gestured to the spare chair he kept tucked under the desk. "Can I sit?"

"Whatever." His frown teetered on the edge of a pout. He crossed his arms. "It's not like I want to be late. But I can't get it to work. I need more time."

"I understand that. But maybe we can brainstorm ways to get there without an extension."

Because the customer was going to be unhappy if she had to go to them for an extension. They were already unhappy with performance on this contract—even if it wasn't actually her team's fault. The previous contractors hadn't pushed back when the client tried to add requirements at the last minute, but ultimately, that was part of why they were no longer doing the work. Stephanie wasn't going to go there. So she pushed back and required new statements of work whenever the scope started to creep. It didn't make her any friends with the client, but the management here was pleased. She'd take it. "Would another pair of hands and eyes be any use?"

Rick tossed his arms in the air. "I don't know. Maybe. But it'll take time to bring them up to speed. It's not like I haven't asked around for some help."

"Who'd you ask?"

"Christopher. Kent. Jerome."

She waited. He was silent. "Just those three?"

"They were all too busy to help, so I figured that was what I'd find from everyone."

Stephanie worked to keep her expression blank as she nodded slowly. "We do have limited resources. What about Danica?"

"What about her?"

"She could probably help. I know she has a little extra time right now and she has solid programming skills."

Rick muttered something.

"I didn't quite catch that. I know you didn't just say 'for a skirt.' Right?" Stephanie's molars were going to be nonexistent by the end of today if things didn't change. She tried to breathe in and count, but looking at Rick's mutinous expression wasn't helping her stay calm.

"I don't want Danica's help."

"Well, she's available and quite capable, so you're not going to be getting what you want today. What do you need to bring along to catch her up to speed?"

"Everything here in my cube. She can come here." Rick's chin jutted up.

Stephanie flicked a glance at the bikini-clad women draped across muscle cars that were the primary decorations in his cube. HR had already ruled that they were allowable—barely—

so that wasn't a battle she'd win. But Stephanie wasn't going to subject someone else to it. "Bring your laptop and whatever else you need. Her cube is bigger."

"Cause she's a girl and gets babied."

Stephanie slowly stood and looked down at Rick. "Do we have a problem?"

He gave a gusty sigh and popped his laptop out of its dock. "Not like you're going to do anything about it. You girls all stick together."

Stephanie bit back the words that wanted to spew. Oh, she'd like to make him drop and do some pushups, but that was the Army and they weren't there. Unfortunately. She settled for jerking her head in the direction of Danica's cube before marching that way. Stephanie didn't bother to see if he followed. He needed help. Danica could give it.

He'd better follow.

"Hey, Danica." Stephanie tapped on the edge of her cube. "You said you have some free time?"

"Yeah." Danica blew a small bubble, sucked it in, and snapped it. "What's up?"

"Rick needs help."

Danica's eyes rolled, but she kept her mouth shut.

Stephanie managed a tight smile. "He'll get you filled in. The deadline doesn't have much—or really any—flex in it. End of the day Friday it needs to be delivered to QA if we're going to make it."

Danica rubbed her hands together. "I love a challenge."

Stephanie laughed. "There you go."

Rick slapped his laptop down on the desk and slumped into the extra chair in Danica's cube. "It'll be better if you realize fast that you can't help. I need to get this figured out so we meet the deadline."

"Right-o. Friday COB. Stephanie said." How Danica was able

to just let Rick's attitude—and all the other attitudes that were so much like his—roll off her back was something Stephanie didn't get. She needed to. Almost wanted to, although she couldn't really say that, because she shouldn't *have* to have a way to deal with their attitudes in the twenty-first century.

"All right. I'll leave the two of you to it. Give me an update at the end of the day so I know if we need to do more." Stephanie made sure to meet Danica's gaze before leaving the cube. Hopefully, if Rick got to be too annoying, Danica would document and report it. That guy needed to go. There were a handful of people—men, like Christopher—who said Rick was good at his job and needed to be kept because he had a wife and kids to support. Even if he had some little quirks.

Little quirks.

Stephanie closed her office door and started her breathing again.

Calling Rick's attitude a "little quirk" was like saying she had some minor scarring on her arm.

Danica could handle him. And she'd handle the problem he was having, most likely. So for now, Stephanie needed to push that task into the "solved" column and move on to the next.

She returned to her desk and logged back in to find out just what the next item needed to be. If nothing else, her work was never boring.

At least the conflict here was unlikely to land her back in the hospital.

CHRISTOPHER EYED the email from Stephanie in his inbox. He hadn't opened it when it came in. The preview showed an acknowledgement of the task assignments, but he knew her. There'd be at least one dig, maybe more, in there. Better to deal with those now, when he was about ready to close up for the day and head home. At least then he could sweat out the inevitable anger during his workout and then reply calmly.

Christopher—

Sounds good. Still think we should get together to combine/refine before meeting with Tyler. I'm open Thursday at 2 or Friday at 11. ~S

He sighed.

He didn't *want* to meet with her. Why couldn't they just work next to each other and get the job done? Except . . . she was probably right.

Darn it.

He pulled up his calendar on his phone and bobbed his head side to side. Thursday or Friday? He could do either one, but letting her know that was probably a bad plan. She'd made a snarky comment—and okay, she hadn't in this email, so maybe she was working on reining it in—and then he'd get all annoyed. He hated being annoyed.

He winced. He could hear his mom in his head reminding him that he was the only one responsible for his response to another person. And fine, true, but still. Ugh. Why did Mom have to be right all the time?

He shifted back to his email and tapped out a quick reply confirming Friday morning. The closer to the deadline for Tyler, the better. She couldn't make him completely redo all his work when they were pushing so close to time. His conscience twinged. She was doing better—clearly trying. He needed to give her grace and the benefit of the doubt.

But that still didn't mean he was ready to move the meeting to Thursday.

Christopher checked the time and quickly shut down his machine. He didn't want to be late to the Bible study he and his best friend, Ryan Foster, hosted at their house on Monday nights. It had started as just the two of them. Roommate bonding plus that extra nudge of accountability that they both needed. Gradually, it had morphed as Ryan—and it really was mostly Ryan—had found other guys to invite.

Was it odd that they all worked for Robinson Enterprises? Maybe—but it wasn't as if they were all in the same arm. He loaded his laptop into its bag, grabbed the folders he needed to take home in case he had a little time to look at them before bed, and hit the lights on his way out of his office.

He was in charge of food tonight. Looked like it was going to be a big bucket of chicken and all the fixings, because that was on the way home and he hadn't planned well enough to avoid the major rush-hour traffic. As it was, what should be a twenty-minute drive was probably going to take at least twice that. That was the joy of living in the DC area. Traffic made everything harder than it should be.

With a wave to the admin who guarded the entrance to the floor, Christopher pushed through the glass doors into the elevator lobby. A couple of the programmers were hanging around, waiting. The "down" light glowed.

"Heading home?"

He turned, pushing his lips into a smile and praying he didn't come across snide. Because Stephanie brought out the snide in him. "Yep. You?"

She nodded and hitched her bag higher on her shoulder. "I'll probably start on the five-year after dinner, but it's nicer at home."

"Really is. If you need me to look at anything before Friday, feel free to email it to me."

Stephanie stiffened. "I think I can handle it."

He winced. "I didn't mean you couldn't. I was trying . . . you know what, never mind."

She pressed her lips together. After a moment, she nodded. "Same goes."

What did she mean?

His confusion must have been visible, because she added, "If you'd like me to look at something, send it my way."

"Oh. Yeah, thanks. I might do that." He'd make a point of it, now. He kept sticking his foot in it with her, and if they were going to get along well enough for him to prove that he should get this promotion, then he needed to make the first move. Maybe she was the test. If he could prove that he could make friends with someone like Stephanie, maybe Joe would see that Christopher had what it took to run the Government Services Group. He'd have to think on that.

The elevator dinged twice before the doors slid open. There were already a handful of people on board, and the group that had been waiting before he showed up all crowded in. One of the guys in the car tilted his head to the side. "You coming?"

"No. I'll wait. Thanks." He glanced at Stephanie. "You want to grab it? I'm sure they'll make room."

"No, that's okay." She shook her head.

The doors slid closed.

Christopher counted to five in his head before pushing the Down button again. He'd finally learned to make himself count so it didn't just open the doors on the full car again. He tucked his hands into his pockets and wondered if there was any small talk that would make standing there with Stephanie less awkward.

"Are you taking work home?" She nodded toward his bag.

He touched the strap. "Oh. Sorta? I don't usually have time on Monday nights."

Her eyebrows lifted. "Standing date night?"

Christopher laughed. He hadn't been on a date in a year. Almost exactly. And he didn't have any plans to go on one any time soon. "No. Men's Bible study."

"Yeah? Cool. Not what I imagined."

"Because?"

She shrugged. "I guess you didn't strike me as a believer."

"Ouch." Another elevator arrived. Christopher nearly laughed again because this one was empty. He gestured for Stephanie to go first. "After you."

"Thanks." Stephanie waited until he was on before pressing the button for the parking garage level. "Where do you go to church?"

Christopher mentioned the name, then added, "I love Pastor Brown's sermons. I'll admit it's been more challenging to find a small group, but I'm still trying them out here and there. Now that our Bible study has grown, I guess I figure maybe we've made our own."

She nodded.

"You?"

"You won't believe me."

"Why not?"

"Because I go to the same church. I guess when there are close to five thousand members and six Sunday services, it's not too surprising that we haven't run into each other, but it's still kind of funny." She snapped her mouth shut as the elevator stopped and the doors slid open to let more people on.

What were the odds? Well, okay, it was one of the three huge churches in the area, so maybe they were larger than he'd imagined. And yet. Of course, Joe attended there as well, and Christopher had never seen the company owner, either. Maybe it was more surprising that Stephanie was a believer—she certainly didn't seem to practice control of her tongue. Maybe he ought to mention the book of James as a study possibility.

Or maybe he ought to deal with the log in his own eye.

He fought a groan. How many times was the Holy Spirit going to have to thwap him on the head about how he thought about—and interacted with—Stephanie? Probably a handful of times more. But he'd keep working on it.

The elevator finally stopped on the garage level. Stephanie's long stride had her halfway across the aisle before Christopher made his way off. He jogged to catch up. *Why, though? Just let her go.*

"Have a good night."

She looked at him, her steps slowing slightly. Stephanie frowned. "Okay. You, too."

Christopher amped up the brightness of his smile a few watts and saluted.

"Ugh. Don't. Not like that."

Heat crept up his neck. "Right. Forgot that's actually a thing you know about. Sorry."

"Just . . . it's a big deal. And it probably shouldn't be to me. So you do you. I'll get over it." She turned and angled toward a military-green Jeep. Then she stopped and twisted back around. "At least keep your wrist straight?"

"Got it. Sorry." Christopher waved. He wasn't going to worry about keeping his wrist straight, because he wasn't going to salute her again. The sketchy two-fingers to his head thing was fine with normal people, but of course it made Stephanie twitchy. Like everything did. He shook his head and tugged on the handle of his silver sedan. The car beeped once and he opened the door. He tossed his coat and laptop bag on the passenger seat before sliding behind the wheel.

Chicken and sides.

Get home.

Study the Bible with people who made sense.

That was a much saner to-do list than spending any more time trying to understand or unravel the mystery of Stephanie Collins.

And it wasn't as if he needed to do that. He just had to work with her for six months and win this promotion.

After that, she could go her merry way and he'd go his.

That was definitely better than trying to make her a friend.

He just needed to keep her from becoming an enemy.

3

Ryan glanced up from the couch when Christopher walked in and laughed. "Knew it."

"Yeah, well." Christopher shrugged. He dropped his work bag by the door and carried the giant tub of chicken and the rest of the food through to the kitchen. "You can't tell me you're not scrambling with the whole contest thing."

Ryan wandered into the kitchen and peeked into the bag of sides. He snagged a fry. "I'm teamed up with your sister. How hard can it be?"

Christopher frowned. How had he forgotten that Jess was paired with Ryan? "How'd that even happen?"

"She's good at her job. Really good. Why'd you send in her résumé and suggest her if you didn't know that?" Ryan reached for another fry.

Christopher snatched the bag. "Stop, man. Wait for everyone to get here. And I don't know, because it was better than letting my sister be unemployed and, oh yeah, in jail."

"Minor detail." Ryan turned and got plates out of the cabinet. "I was thinking, though."

"Uh-oh."

"Now you stop. What if we invited Tyler to join the Bible study? Then we'd have all of the guys in the contest."

"Shaw? You want to invite Shaw?"

"Why not? Pretty sure he's a believer—he'd have to be if he's that close with Joe, don't you think?"

Christopher shook his head. Tyler's spiritual status was the last of his concerns with inviting the guy to join them. Why couldn't Ryan see that? "He's in charge of this contest. We already have to send our drafts for him to look over—what if we have prayer requests about how things are going? You really think giving him that kind of inside information is smart?"

Ryan raised his eyebrows. "Wow. You're really serious about winning."

"Aren't you?"

Ryan blew out a breath. "Yeah, I guess. But I mean if Jess is the better person for the job, then that's fine, too. She'd be great —you have to know that—so it feels like I win either way."

Christopher studied his friend. "How can you be so laid back? We're talking about the chance to *run* a major corporation here and everything that goes into that. Prestige, contacts, salary, perks . . . we could buy a house instead of this apartment."

"Yeah, if I buy a house, I'm not sharing it with you." Ryan frowned. "I don't know. I'm doing okay right now. I make good money. I have a place I like and friends. Maybe more would be fun, but there have to be downsides to it."

"Do there?" None came to mind right away. Even just being in charge was enough to keep Christopher all in. It'd be nice to be the one making all the decisions, not just following behind where others had led.

"If there weren't, do you think Joe would be doing this?" Ryan pointed at Christopher. "Seriously, think about that. He's been married to this company for what, thirty years? Now he wants to get married for real and he's breaking everything up to make sure he has time for what matters. I don't think we should overlook that. Don't you want to get married? Start a family?"

Christopher blew out a breath. "Yeah. But I don't think they necessarily exclude each other."

Ryan opened his mouth.

Christopher held up a hand. "I hear you, though. I'll keep it in mind."

Ryan's face still held traces of a scowl, but he nodded.

The door buzzer sounded.

"I'll go get it."

He watched as Ryan strode from the kitchen. Christopher shook his head and turned back to the food to continue unloading onto the island. He wasn't motivated by the wrong things, was he? The management—or mis-management as far as he was concerned—was a problem in their arm of the company. Was it wrong to do better? To do it right?

Maybe it was a little conceited to think he could. He preferred to consider it self-confidence, rather than ego. And that was something Stephanie would say. Maybe the two of them were more alike than he realized?

Ugh. What a depressing thought.

Ryan came back with Aaron Powell following behind.

"It's always bucket chicken when you're in charge, man. Why is that?" Aaron reached for a fry, stopping when Ryan laughed. "What?"

"Nothing. That sounds like Ian." Ryan turned and left the kitchen.

Christopher pointed to the stack of plates. "If you're going to eat, why not do it properly."

"Yes, ma'am." Aaron smirked as he reached for a plate and started loading it.

"Chicken night." Ian came into the kitchen rubbing his hands together. "I've been looking forward to this all weekend."

"It might not have been chicken." Christopher stepped away from the island to make room for the others to fill their plates. He crossed his arms. "Sometimes I cook."

"I can't think of the last time it was your turn for food and it wasn't chicken. More than a year, for sure." Aaron put a large scoop of neon-orange mac and cheese on his plate. "It's okay, man. No one minds."

"Sure seems like it." Christopher could hear the bad temper in his mutter. He took the last plate and started adding food as the rest of the guys headed into the living room.

Ryan hung back. "You okay?"

"Not really, since, apparently, I'm a materialistic jerk who never cares enough to make real food and predictably provides poultry instead."

Ryan snickered.

"What?" Christopher slammed his plate down on the island. "That's funny to you?"

Ryan sobered. "Not the content, but come on. Predictably provides poultry?"

Christopher's lips twitched. He fought them back into a frown.

"Christopher, get a grip. This is what we do. You know Aaron always makes spaghetti with plain marinara. He wouldn't know a meat sauce if it bit him on the behind. And with Ian, it's always some kind of burger." Ryan shrugged. "It is what it is."

"And you?" Christopher picked up his plate and added a scoop of green beans to it. They weren't particularly healthy, having been stewed to death in ham bone juice, but they were green. That had to count for something.

Ryan flashed a grin. "I'm creative and inspired in the kitchen, so obviously I do the best job of all of us when it's my turn."

Christopher snorted out a laugh.

Ryan clasped a hand to his chest. "Ouch. You wound me."

"I'd like to wound you." Christopher jabbed his elbow into Ryan's side as he passed. He found a spot in the living room and sat. "Hey, guys. Ryan says that since he's better in the kitchen, he's doing food each week until the contest is over."

"Nice, bro!" Aaron held up his hand for a high five.

"Wait. What?" Ryan shook his head. "I didn't say—"

"Yeah. Take-and-bake meals from Costco." Ian slapped Aaron's hand. "A lot of rotisserie chicken in there, but they mix it up. Can we have the pot pie next week?"

Ryan's cheeks flamed red. "You know they're from Costco?"

"You didn't think we'd notice the container lids?" Christopher shook his head. "Dude."

Ryan hunched his shoulders and sagged into his seat. "Fine. Pot pies next week. But if I'm cooking, you're all pitching in on the cost."

"Seems fair." Aaron reached into his pocket for his wallet and tossed a twenty-dollar bill onto the coffee table. "That should cover a month, right?"

Christopher eyed the money. It seemed about right. He dug out a twenty of his own and added it to the pile.

Ian followed suit.

With a sigh, Ryan collected the cash and stuffed it in his pocket. "Who's saying the blessing? We should eat and get to the study."

Christopher hid a grin. This group of guys never failed to lift his spirits. Even when they were the ones who dampened them in the first place. "I will. Let's pray."

His prayer was short and to the point, but silently he added on a prayer for discernment and wisdom. And clarity when it came to his motives. He didn't want to get caught in the trap of chasing after money. Or power. Or prestige.

But was it wrong to have those things—to want them? Even if the plan was to use them for good?

"Okay, we're in Mark eight this week. Who's reading?" Christopher shifted his plate to one knee and set his phone, the Bible app open to the passage, on the other.

"I can." Ian leaned forward and set his almost-empty plate on the coffee table.

Christopher listened as Ian read about Jesus healing a blind man and Peter declaring that Jesus was the Christ. They were working their way through the whole New Testament. Part of him loved it, but sometimes it was hard. The stories were familiar. Was there going to be anything to discuss? Anything new?

"What good is it for someone to gain the whole world and yet forfeit their soul?" Ian kept reading to the end of the chapter, but Christopher froze.

He tapped the verse and selected a highlight color. He'd read it before. Heard it. But those were all at a time when he wasn't in a position to gain the whole world.

Now that he was? The words were convicting.

STEPHANIE TOOK her laptop off the dock and reached for her mug of coffee. She and Christopher hadn't said where they were meeting to go over everything before submitting the final version to Tyler, but knowing him, he'd expect her to come to him.

Whatever.

She could reach out and suggest her space, but he'd probably decide she meant more by it than simply wanting to make a choice that gave them both more room. His office wasn't so much smaller that it was worth getting into whatever morass of issues that would cause.

At least not to her.

She hadn't sent him any of her pieces ahead of time even

though he'd passed a couple of his her way. She'd returned each of them within a couple of hours with suggestions and tweaks—hopefully, he agreed she'd made them better.

Stephanie took a deep breath and blew it out. No sense in getting agitated about something she didn't know for sure would happen. Even if it seemed likely.

She was good at her job. Joe wouldn't have included her in this contest if she weren't capable of handling the prize. Christopher needed to keep that at the front of his mind. It never paid to underestimate the competition.

She tapped on his half-open door.

"Come in."

Stephanie pushed the door the rest of the way open. "You ready?"

Christopher glanced up, a slight frown creating wrinkles between his eyebrows. "Is it already time?"

"I'm a few minutes late, actually. Sorry."

"Everything okay?"

Stephanie managed a little shrug. "It's fine. Just personality problems."

He nodded like it was no big deal. Maybe to him it wasn't, but dealing with Danica and Rick was going to drive her insane. Rick was . . . no words came to mind that were things she should be saying. *Made in God's image.* That was what she needed to remember.

"Okay. Um, how did you want to do this?" Christopher scooted his chair to the side so he wasn't blocked by his monitor.

"I guess just merge everything into one document that we can submit to Tyler." She shrugged. "Did you have a different idea?"

"No. That's fine. Do you want to send me yours or have me send you mine?"

"Why don't you send me yours and I'll paste mine in?"

Stephanie glanced around his office for a place to set up. He didn't have an extra table in here—there was just his desk. She gestured to the end of the L-shaped workstation. "Can I work right there?"

"Sure. I get to read it through before you send it to Tyler. Right?"

It galled that he'd ask. Did he think she was such a horrible person that she was going to submit something that reflected on their future without letting him see it? "Would you rather do the pasting? I don't have to. Although I guess I'd then ask the same thing—to be able to read it over first."

Christopher's cheeks reddened and he looked away. "Sorry."

"Are you going to be able to do this?"

"Do what?" He kept his gaze on his monitor as he worked the mouse.

Her email dinged with an incoming message, but she watched Chris. "Work with me. You hate me. I get it. Most everyone does. That's fine. But if you can't or won't believe that I'm going to treat you professionally, then maybe we need to go talk to Joe and see what he thinks is the right solution."

Chris's head jerked up and he met her gaze, startled. "He'd remove both of us and choose two new contenders."

"Probably." It wasn't what she wanted. She wanted to win this. But she also didn't want to spend the next six months working with someone who was looking for opportunities to deride her.

"You'd be okay with that?"

"No. But it's better than being treated badly for the next six months."

"I don't think it was out of line to ask." He crossed his arms.

Of course he didn't. Because she was Stephanie Collins and everyone knew she was a horrible person who didn't ever deserve even the barest shred of common courtesy. Her eyes burned, but she ignored it. She hadn't cried when she was in the Army. She wasn't going to cry in an office job. Instead, she shifted to her email, ignoring the bold, unread messages. She opened a new email, clicked the paperclip, and scrolled to her planning document. When it was attached, she tapped in Chris's address in the "To" field and hit Send. "You go ahead and do the pasting. I'd appreciate at least being copied on the final submission to Tyler."

"Steph—"

She shook her head and stood, slapping the lid of her laptop closed before tucking it under her arm. "I have personnel problems to deal with that I can't ignore. At least this one is easily solved."

"I didn't mean . . ."

She didn't know if he quit talking or she just stopped being able to hear him when she walked out of the office and pulled his door closed behind her.

She also didn't care. Let him think what he wanted. It didn't bother her. She wasn't going to let it.

Stephanie strode back to her office, dropped her laptop onto its dock and stared out the window. She definitely wasn't in the right frame of mind to go try to deal with Rick. She'd end up doing or saying something that would leave Chris smirking and saying "I told you so" to himself and all his buddies.

She knew he talked about her to his cronies.

That was just one more thing she wasn't going to worry about. Right now, she was going to take a walk. She grabbed her phone and her coat and headed for the stairwell. Jogging down the stairs was soothing. Her frustration with Chris and Rick slowly started to fade, replaced by numbers.

There were fifteen steps on each flight of stairs. Two flights between each floor. Eight floors to the ground level exit. Halfway down, she began to alternate, counting up to fifteen on one flight, then back down to one on the next. By the time she reached the lobby, her breathing was slightly labored, but at least her psyche was calm.

She walked to the revolving door and out into the cold January air. The sharp bite of wind racing around the corner of a nearby building was nice after the workout of the stairs. She kept her jacket over her arm as she turned and started down the short side of the building. Maybe she wouldn't need to do the full four-block walk that she had mapped out for her breaks. She really did need to get back and deal with Rick and Danica.

Her phone buzzed.

Groaning, she looked at the screen and nearly laughed. Danica.

Stephanie swiped up to answer the call. "Hey, Danica."

"Stephanie, you have to fix Rick."

She managed to turn her snort into a cough-slash-throat-clear. "I'm going to speak to him. I needed a quick break before I did."

"That's something, at least." Danica sighed. "Why is he like this?"

"Because he knows he's terrible at his job and doesn't like being called out." Stephanie waited at the corner for the light to change before hurrying across. "That's my best guess."

"I don't understand how he's still employed. Can't you do something about that?"

"We have to follow the process. It's there for everyone's protection."

"So you're just going to write him up again and he'll moan about how you have it out for him and that's why he didn't get the promotion he deserved, and nothing will change? I thought you were better than that. It's why I wanted to transfer to your department."

Stephanie held her tongue. She'd already said too much. "I appreciate your helping him out."

"Yeah, well. I'm not sure how much good it did. He doesn't like my changes even though they fixed his code. He says he isn't going to leave them in, but will use them as inspiration to fix it himself."

Stephanie pinched the bridge of her nose and turned back toward the office. She wasn't going to be able to complete her walk, after all. "I'll be there in a few minutes. That's due to QA by close of business today. Did you save a working copy?"

"Yeah, I have it backed up."

"You're a lifesaver, Danica."

"Tell it to my annual review."

Stephanie smiled slightly. "I'll make a note."

"Is there anything you can do about Rick? I'm tired of picking up his slack."

"I know. I'll see what I can figure out. Thanks again." Stephanie ended the call and hurried back across the street toward her building. Didn't Rick understand deadlines at all? The contracts weren't guidelines. There were penalties for missing. They were cutting it close to the wire as it was—and she didn't like that at all. In a perfect world, his portion would have been submitted last Friday so QA could have two full weeks to poke at it. Now they were down to one, and if the test cases weren't written well enough to ensure all major functionality was accounted for? The code would go into production and the customer would break it. And then someone's head would roll.

Stephanie really didn't want that head to be hers.

She jogged through the revolving door and into the lobby, and checked the time on her phone. She'd been gone a little over ten minutes. The stairs would take less time, probably, but she'd arrive sweaty and out of breath. She needed to be together when she cornered Rick. She pushed the Up button for the elevator and drummed her fingers on her leg while she waited for the car to arrive.

What was she going to do about Rick?

Stephanie got off on her floor and swung by her office to drop off her coat. She still wasn't sure of the right words to use to get Rick to understand that the working program—the one that Danica had fixed—was getting submitted now, not after he'd had time to dink around with it anymore.

"There you are." Rick scowled at her, looming in her doorway. "Where've you been?"

"Excuse me?" Stephanie straightened and gestured to one of her visitor chairs. If he wanted to have this conversation here, then that was what they'd do.

He hunched his shoulders slightly as he stomped to the chair. "I needed to talk to you and couldn't find you."

"Your project isn't my only priority right now." Stephanie took the chair behind her desk and cleared her throat. "Did you get things working?"

"Danica says she fixed it. I need another week though. I'm not convinced her code is right. So I want to go through it more closely and—"

Stephanie held up her hand. "Let me go ahead and save some time. No."

"But—"

"Rick. No. We've already shaved a week off the QA process. The code needs to get sent now, and you need to get started on the development of the next deliverable so our week delay doesn't spiral. Danica says it's working now. You agreed that it's working. So we're going to move on."

"She's not even on this project. She doesn't know if it's working or not." He leaned forward, his eyebrows drawn together. "This is *my* deliverable. I deserve to have the chance to make sure it's right."

Stephanie had to fight not to cut him off again. Now she was glad she hadn't. "You want to do the testing? I know they're short staffed in QA, so if that's something you're interested in, a lateral transfer will be very easy to arrange. I didn't realize that was your preference. I'm so sorry that I didn't ask you and make this happen sooner. No wonder you're upset."

"No. I—that's not—" Rick snapped his mouth shut and glowered at her. "I'll get the code submitted to QA and get started on the next deliverable."

"Copy me and Danica on the submission, please. Just so we can check all the boxes."

"You don't trust me to submit the right files?"

Stephanie offered a tight smile. "Was there anything else?"

"No." He stood, frowned at her, and stalked from her office.

Stephanie blew out a breath. She'd reach out to the QA director anyway. If they could use Rick, she'd be happy to have him gone. He had to be more capable of testing software than he was at writing it.

"Knock knock." Christopher poked his head in and smiled. "Got a sec?"

She wanted to groan but gestured for him to come ahead. She scribbled a note about QA and verifying the deliverable with Danica before glancing at Christopher. "What's up?"

"I submitted the plan to Tyler. He wants to meet with us."

"That was fast." She bit her lip. It had to be bad for him to want to talk to them already, didn't it? "Did he say when?"

Christopher winced. "Now?"

"Great." Stephanie didn't bother to sigh. She stood. "Lead the way."

"Was that Rick I saw leaving?"

She glanced over as they walked toward the bank of elevators. "Yeah. You know him?"

"Only by reputation." His voice conveyed an understanding

that Rick's reputation wasn't one to envy. He pressed the Call button and the doors opened with a chime. "I guess I didn't realize he was on one of your projects."

"Yeah, I got him in a shrewd business deal." Stephanie let the sarcasm drip from her words as she stepped into the elevator. "I think we came to an understanding today, though. He might be better suited to QA."

Christopher's eyebrows lifted. "That's not a bad idea, actually. From what I gather he's good at breaking things."

Stephanie laughed and some of the tension in her shoulder blades eased. "He is that. Did Tyler say anything about why he wanted to see us?"

Christopher shook his head. "You didn't see the email?"

"Not yet. Rick's been taking up my time. How did you get the two documents put into one so fast?" It had been barely over an hour since she'd left his office. If she'd done it, she'd probably still be cutting and pasting—or at least just finishing up now.

"I used the merge function."

She closed her eyes. "Well, that's probably why he wants to see us then."

"What's wrong with merge?"

"Technically nothing, but it's easy to see in the document properties. So he'll know we each did half and then put them together." She shrugged. Maybe that wasn't going to be the problem, but she'd bet a dollar it was.

"Divvying up the work is smart management."

"Save it for the jury." The elevator doors opened on the executive level. Her stomach clenched. She didn't like getting called up here—it was like being sent to the principal's office.

They walked in silence to Tyler's.

"Ah, good. Come on in, you two." Tyler smiled and gestured to the little round table in the corner. "Have a seat."

4

Stephanie slid around the table and took the seat in the corner. She didn't want to. She'd rather have an easy way to escape, but it was better than having her back to the door. Chris took the seat next to hers, blocking her in. It was fine.

She breathed in deeply and ignored the tantalizing scent of Chris's aftershave. Or maybe it was his deodorant. Whatever it was smelled good, and he had no business smelling that amazing.

Tyler sat, crossing his arms on the table. "Tell me a little about the process you used to put together this five-year plan draft."

Stephanie looked over at Chris and lifted her eyebrows.

He cleared his throat. "Well, we thought it was easiest to split it up and each do half, then merge the documents."

"I see. And you were on board with that approach, Stephanie?"

"Not completely? But I also didn't want to make a fuss. When Christopher insisted, I let it go. But not because I wanted to do it a different way so much as I suspected you and Joe wouldn't be happy if we did it the way we did."

Tyler's lips curved slightly. "And you win that bet."

"Why does it matter?" Christopher leaned forward, his expression earnest. "Seriously, why? We got the job done. It's a solid plan with clear, actionable steps and easily measured benchmarks. There are strategies for pivoting if, after time, it looks like we need to try different approaches."

"It has all of that. On the surface, it's a solid draft. I can absolutely give you that accolade. But the point of this competition is to see the two of you working together. No matter who wins, the other will have to be able to work with them—most likely as second in command—"

"Which is why it's good to know that we can delegate and the other will do their part without supervision." Christopher frowned. "Sorry. I don't mean to interrupt. I just don't see why we should waste time sitting together to do this kind of thing."

Tyler sighed. He turned his gaze on Stephanie. "Do you understand?"

Did she? Not really. At the same time, she understood how to follow orders. And working together had definitely been part of their orders. "I understand that it's what we've been asked to do."

Tyler laughed.

Christopher snorted. "You can't bear to agree with me, can you?"

"Seriously?" Stephanie shook her head. "I agree that the way we did it was efficient. But you can't admit that you knew it wasn't what they asked us to do?"

Christopher frowned.

"Did you understand that?" Tyler turned and pinned Christopher with his gaze.

"I guess." Christopher's voice was resigned, edging on pouty.

"Great. Then I'll expect the two of you to spend time together this weekend making this draft shine. You have a good start on content—but it needs to read like a single person wrote it. Even without checking the settings, I would have known the two of you split the work." Tyler smiled and knocked on the table. "If it helps any, you weren't the only ones who did it this way. So unless you have questions, I'll let you get back to work."

"I'm good. Thanks Tyler." Stephanie scooted her chair back and glanced at Christopher. He'd have to leave before she'd be able to get out. Would he get the hint?

"No questions here. I'm sorry. Both of you. I should have listened when Stephanie reminded me of the directive." Chris stood. "If I had, we wouldn't have had to waste your time."

"It's fine. Like I said, you're not the only ones."

Stephanie trailed behind Christopher. She wasn't going to say "I told you so," no matter how much she wanted to.

He jabbed the elevator button then shoved his hands in his pockets.

"You okay?"

Christopher blew out a breath. "I guess. Not exactly the first impression I was hoping to make."

She nodded.

"So. Are you busy tonight?"

Her eyebrows lifted. The elevator arrived, buying her time to think. Tyler had said to work this weekend on the final draft. That was what Christopher meant. It had to be. She stepped inside, waiting for Christopher to join her before poking the button for their floor. "No. I don't have any plans tonight or tomorrow."

Chris scrubbed his hands over his face. "We might as well start tonight. Then at least we'll know how much more time we need. I'd as soon not work on Sunday if we can avoid it."

Stephanie nodded. "That suits me."

"Do you want to come to my place? We can order something in and have a working dinner?"

"Okay." It was better than inviting him to her place. She didn't like strangers in her space. "Text me your address. I can pick something up on the way, if that's easier? I wouldn't mind going home to change first."

"Sure. I'm not picky about the food. If you'd rather bring something, that'll work." Christopher shrugged. The elevator dinged and the doors slid open on their floor. "Would you mind if I ask my roommate if he wants in? He'd pay for his, obviously, but usually we end up going in together."

"You have a roommate. Is he going to mind if I come over?" Should she offer her place? She really didn't want to.

"Nah. For all I know, he won't be home tonight." Chris shrugged. "Or he'll be working with my sister on their five-year plan."

"Right." She'd forgotten his sister was on one of the other teams. "Just let me know."

"Okay." He hesitated.

Stephanie waited. Was he going to say something else, or was she just going to stand there looking stupid?

"Look, I really am sorry. I should have listened to you."

That was unexpected. She'd figured the apology in Tyler's office for a face-saving maneuver. But there was no one to see or hear now. So maybe it was actually genuine. "Accepted. I'll see you tonight."

"Yeah, sounds good. I'll text you the address." He started down the hall toward his office.

Stephanie watched him walk away—he looked good from the back. And from the front. None of which mattered. He didn't like her. She obviously didn't like him. Or find him attractive. Nor was she looking forward to seeing his place and having time alone with him.

Not even a little bit.

She blew out a breath and headed toward her office.

Yeah, right.

"SHE'S COMING HERE?"

Christopher rolled his eyes. Ryan obviously had no intention of letting this go. "Yes. For the sixteenth time. And she's bringing us dinner. I hope you have cash to pay your part."

Ryan scowled. "I can't just shoot it to her electronically?"

"I don't know. I don't know her well enough to know which, if any, of the cash apps she uses. Maybe that's fine." He should have chosen a different location. The public library was open until ten on Friday, wasn't it? They could have snagged a table in one of the collab rooms and dealt with it. Or he could have asked about her place, though since she didn't offer, it probably wasn't an option. And why did he include dinner? This was work. Not a date. Not a working date.

He didn't like her like that.

"Touchy." Ryan batted his eyelashes with an exaggerated sappy expression. "Am I going to be in the way?"

"No. We're working." Chris turned the TV off and tossed the remote onto the coffee table. "Did you and Jess get called into Tyler's office today, too?"

"No. Unlike you, we followed directions."

Christopher scowled. "When did you have time to get together with my sister?"

"Lunch? Downtime at work here and there. Wednesday evening." Ryan shrugged and grabbed a banana out of the bowl on the island that was filled with fruit and assorted kitchen junk. "Guess that's a gold star for us and a black mark for you. Excuse me while I make sad trombone noises."

"Jerk." Christopher's lips twitched. "I appreciate your keeping an eye on my baby sister. I still worry about her."

"No sweat. I really think she's on the straight and narrow these days." Ryan peeled the banana and consumed it in four enormous bites.

"Hungry?"

"I missed lunch today." Ryan tossed the peel in the garbage. "I'll still be able to handle the Thai food she's bringing. You said Thai, right?"

"That's what she said. I told her what you usually ordered." This was such a dumb idea. He shouldn't have invited her here. And dinner? Ryan was supposed to be a buffer, but the way his best friend was acting, he was liable to make it awkward just for the fun of it. "Maybe you should eat in your room."

"No." Ryan pulled a chair away from the table, flipped it around, and straddled it. "Tell you what, Nervous Nellie. I'll eat with you—on my best behavior—and then I'll head down to the gym. I can get in a good workout and then hang in the rec area till what, nine?"

"Nine should work." He'd make sure of it. Even if it meant they had to meet up at the library for the bulk of the day tomorrow. "Thanks."

"Don't thank me. There'll be payback of some sort eventually." Ryan rested his chin on his arms. "If I'd known this was a date, I would've passed on the Thai food."

"It's not a date."

"Keep telling yourself that, bro."

The buzzer cut off Chris's reply. He lurched to his feet and headed toward the door, pointing his finger at Ryan on the way past. "Zip it."

Chris flipped the locks and pulled open the door. For just an instant, his breath caught in his chest.

She smiled. "Hi. Sorry if I'm late."

"No. No, it's fine." He stepped back and gestured for her to come in. *Standing there gawking like an idiot. Smooth. Not a date.* "Come on in. You remember Ryan?"

"Sure. Good to see you again." Stephanie glanced around the condo. "Where should I put all this?"

"Oh. Kitchen. Here let me help you." Chris reached for the takeout bags. "Sorry."

"Thanks. Laptop bag and coat?"

"Maybe just toss them on the couch?" He pointed toward the living room, avoiding Ryan's smirk. His roommate was delusional. And Christopher was probably never going to hear the end of this. Ever. *Fabulous.* "It smells good."

Stephanie crossed to the living room and shrugged out of her coat. She left her things there and wandered to the kitchen. "It's my favorite Thai place. There are a couple that are good near the office, but this one is best."

"Yeah?" Ryan cocked his head and squinted at the bags. "I'm always on the lookout for better Thai. You're generous to the ones near the office."

Stephanie chuckled. "Beggars and choosers, you know?"

Ryan nodded.

"Neither of you specified heat levels so I left it the way they put it on the menu." Stephanie pulled her lip between her teeth. "Which can be a little hotter than you might be expecting."

"Hotter the better." Ryan grinned and stood, flipping his chair back around. "I'll get the cutlery."

At least he was finally going to do something other than make things awkward. Chris unloaded the containers. Why were there so many of them?

"I got spring rolls. And dumplings. They're appetizers and so yummy, but if you don't want any, I'll just take them home. They reheat pretty well and it's better than a Lean Cuisine for lunch."

She crossed her arms. "I wasn't expecting you to chip in on those."

"I don't mind. They sound good. Did you want to use plates or just eat out of the containers?" His hands were suddenly sweaty. He wiped them on his jeans.

Ryan turned a laugh into a cough. "I'll get plates. Might as well pretend we're civilized, right?"

"Sure. But I'm not fussy." Stephanie tugged open the lids and pushed the main entrees around. "What you ordered should be closest to you."

"Great." Chris turned and took the stack of plates from Ryan. He handed one to Stephanie and kept one for himself before giving the third back to his roomie. He picked up his entrée and set it on top of his plate, then frowned.

Ryan laughed. "You just want to eat out of the container. Admit it."

Christopher shrugged. "Kinda. I'm not big on sharing food."

Stephanie's lips quirked up. "I'm not, either, but I was going to pretend. We can still use the plates for the dumplings and spring rolls."

"That works." Ryan dropped his container onto his plate and reached for one of the appetizers.

Christopher followed suit and nodded toward the dining table. "Go ahead and get situated. Do you want a soda?"

"Sure. That'll work. Thanks."

"Preference?"

Stephanie shook her head and set her plate on the table before pulling out a chair and sitting. "Whatever you have is fine."

"Ry?"

"Sure. Why not?" Ryan moved into the dining room.

Christopher frowned and detoured to the fridge for drinks.

When he got to the table, Ryan and Stephanie were laughing. "I missed the joke?"

"She was telling me about Rick. You remember Rick?"

"Ugh. Yes. Did you get that mess with him today figured out?" Christopher popped the top of his soda.

"We'll have to see. QA doesn't want him, though. His reputation has already made the rounds." She shrugged. "So we'll have to see what happens."

Christopher nodded. It was a problem. Thankfully, though, it wasn't his problem. For all that he'd been selected to compete, technically Stephanie was his boss. Which right now was a good thing. "Should we say grace?"

"Sure." Stephanie folded her hands and bowed her head.

Christopher glanced at Ryan, who shook his head slightly. Great. Fine. He could pray. Even if it was weird with Stephanie here. He said something short to bless the food and not much else. It probably made a worse impression than if he'd just skipped it all together. What was it about her that had him constantly second guessing?

They ate quickly with friendly, inconsequential conversation. Much of that was because the food was some of the best Thai he'd had in . . . ever? So it was nice to keep his head down and focus on the spicy noodles.

"I'll get the dishes. Then I think I'm going to head down to the gym and let the two of you work without distractions. Thanks for bringing dinner, Stephanie." Ryan collected the empty containers and dirty plates and headed into the kitchen.

"I wouldn't have minded helping." Stephanie frowned after Ryan. "And he doesn't have to leave. I—"

"It's okay." Christopher held up a hand. "This was his plan before you came. He likes to work out on Fridays when he doesn't have a date."

"All right. I just don't like the idea that I'm inconveniencing someone in their own home."

Did she not mind if it wasn't in their home? He tried to stop the snarky thought before it finished, but failed. He cleared his throat. "If you want to grab your laptop, it's probably easier to work at the table. Would you like another soda?"

"Maybe just some water?"

"Sure. Ice?"

"No, thanks." Stephanie stood and headed to the living room.

Chris watched her for a moment before giving himself a firm shake and moving to the kitchen for drinks.

Ryan was putting the last dish in the dishwasher. He smirked at Christopher. "My plan, huh?"

"Yeah, well. She felt bad." He kept his voice low. "You didn't want her to insist you stay, did you?"

"No. I'm good." Ryan rinsed his hands, dried them, and hung the towel on the edge of the sink. "Later, man. Be good."

"What's that supposed to mean?"

Ryan just waggled his eyebrows as he danced backwards out of the room.

Oh, ick. There was no danger of not being good. Chris fought a shudder as he reached for the door to the cabinet where the glasses were stored. Sure, she was decent looking. Maybe hot, depending on the angle. But her personality. Uh-uh. Stephanie was not the kind of woman he was looking for.

Plus, she was his boss.

And they were in competition for this senior position.

If he won, he'd be her boss.

It was just a bad idea all around.

He filled the glasses from the door of the fridge and went back to the dining room table. Of course now the question was where to sit. They were supposed to work together, which probably meant he needed to sit beside her. But . . . ugh. This was like middle school. *Grow up, Chris.*

Stephanie reached for her water. "Thanks. How did you want to do this?"

"I guess sit together and work through it from the top?"

She nodded and set her laptop down, then sat.

Chris took the chair beside her. He sipped his water. "Do you mind running the computer? I can get mine if you'd rather I did."

"No, this is fine. I can drive." She clicked a few times and brought up their document.

He scooted a bit closer so he could see and made the mistake of breathing in her perfume. It wasn't a strong scent—he'd never noticed it before. He'd never been this close to her before. But it was light and made him picture a summer meadow full of wild-flowers.

"You ready?" She turned her head and his gaze locked with hers. She had little gold rings around her pupils.

His breath froze in his chest. She was pretty.

He didn't need to know that.

It was just one more thing he'd have to fight. He schooled his features into a relaxed smile, praying she couldn't see through it. "Sure. Let's do this."

5

Christopher checked the time and shifted gears. In the last two and a half weeks, he and Stephanie had been getting along a lot better—but he still wasn't going to be late to one of their meetings. Since Tyler continued to make it clear that collaboration meant a whole bunch of togetherness, he and Stephanie had arranged to meet at the end of each day for thirty minutes. Then, if they had additional tasks that they weren't able to complete that way, they'd spend the weekend on it.

It was working, but it was also making it increasingly hard for him to stop noticing things like her perfume and the way she filled out her work clothes. She might not be in the Army anymore, but it was clear she kept fit.

He had no business noticing anything like that about her.

Even if he did, it didn't mean he liked her. She was still the overly blunt woman she'd been since he met her.

He undocked his laptop and tucked it under his arm before heading out of his office toward Stephanie's.

Raised voices carried through the carpeted corridor. He couldn't quite make out the words, though they became clearer as he walked. He winced. That was definitely Stephanie, and while she might not technically be yelling, her voice definitely carried. And it was firm.

"No, Rick, *you* don't understand. That's not how deadlines work. I'm sorry that you're just now realizing that, given that you say you've been in the workforce for more than fifteen years."

Yikes.

Christopher slowed his steps. He didn't want to interrupt. Except maybe he could help out somehow? Not that she'd appreciate that. Still, Rick could be a pain to work with, but he seemed like a decent enough guy.

"You can't talk to me that way."

"Sit down, Rick. We're not finished."

"Yes, we are. I'm going up to talk to Joe. Then we'll see who's right and who's you."

"Knock knock." Christopher tapped on Stephanie's door with a tentative smile. "Am I late?"

"No. But I need another minute if you don't mind waiting. Maybe you could close the door. Rick and I need to finish this conversation." Stephanie's smile was tight and her eyes were lit with fury.

"Don't listen to her. We're done. So is she. No one treats me this way." Rick stood, scowling at Stephanie, and started to push past Christopher.

"Can I help?" He didn't back down. Rick could get out, but he'd have to be more physical than Christopher thought was likely.

"Sure. You can explain to this little girl that contract deadlines aren't the hard and fast entities she seems to think they are. Clients would rather have things perfect a week or two late than get something rushed and on time." Rick made finger quotes as he spoke the last two words. He rolled his eyes as he nodded toward Stephanie. "She doesn't seem to get that. Which is why skirts—"

"Let me go ahead and stop you there." Christopher held up a hand. Behind Rick, Stephanie was visibly fuming. Had the man no sense?

"Right, right. Not where she can hear. Not that it matters, right?"

"Oh, it matters." Christopher paused and took a deep breath. "There are a lot of things wrong with what you just said, but let's focus on the ones that matter most to the business. Deadlines are not flexible or squishy guidelines. I don't know where you got that idea, but you're wrong. Part of what you said was right."

Rick turned to smirk at Stephanie. "See?"

"Customers *do* expect us to deliver software that's perfect. And they expect it on or before the contractual deadline."

"Which is what I've been trying to explain to him for the last forty-five minutes." Stephanie's words came through clenched teeth.

Rick looked back and forth between Stephanie and Christopher. He snorted. "I see how it is."

"Do you?" Christopher frowned. "I really wish I believed that."

"Yeah, well, you'll be wishing for more than that when I'm done talking to Joe. The only change is, now I'm reporting both of you, not just her. Hope you've got your job searching hats dusted off. I'm sure going to enjoy watching you both carry boxes down to the garage. Now, if you'll excuse me." Rick knocked into Christopher's shoulder, making him crack his head against the door jamb.

"Are you all right?" Stephanie didn't move from where she stood behind her desk. Her hands were bunched into fists, and her chest rose and fell more rapidly than it should.

Christopher rubbed the side of his head. "Yeah. You?"

"Fine. And I could have handled him."

His eyebrows lifted. He hadn't expected her to thank him, but really? She was going to get annoyed that he'd stepped in? "Sure."

She narrowed her eyes, shot a finger at him, and picked up the handset on her desk phone.

What was she doing? He shrugged and moved to the little table in the front corner of her office. He'd be ready to work when she was. Meanwhile, there was always email.

"Yeah, hi, Salil, it's Stephanie." She sank slowly back into the chair at her desk. "I figured I'd let you know that things with Rick are going to come to a head sooner rather than later."

Chris flipped open his laptop and tried not to listen in, although it was basically impossible. It was good that she was talking to HR. At least, he assumed it was Salil in HR. It was possible there was more than one man with that name in the company, but it seemed unlikely. Especially if she was talking about Rick, because HR would've been his first call, too. Of course, he wasn't convinced he would have ended up in the same position Stephanie was in. He had better people skills.

"That's right. At least this time, I have a witness to his belligerence and sexism. Christopher Ward arrived toward the end of the conversation and attempted to intervene." She paused, nodding as Salil must have been speaking. "That's correct."

He fought the urge to close his eyes. He didn't want to be involved at the HR level. He'd have to mention that he'd heard Stephanie's voice raised from down the hall. And sure, Rick had crossed the line with his comments, but how long had she been picking at him before he finally exploded?

"Okay. Yes, he said he was on his way to Joe." Stephanie cleared her throat, but it sounded suspiciously like she was hiding a snicker. "Right. Thanks. Let me know, okay?"

Christopher waited while she hung up the phone and pressed her fingers to her eyes. Okay, so she wasn't completely unaffected. And still, Rick wasn't the only one who'd been unprofessional. His stomach sank—there was no way anything he said or did was going to go over well.

"Okay." She took a deep breath and blew it out. "That's done and hopefully the last that I'll have to deal with Rick. You're ready?"

"Yeah. I took a little time this morning researching open proposals that still have enough time for us to consider bidding. They're all a little bit of a stretch—we might need to find a sub here or there to round out the capabilities—but that would help grow our area of effectiveness."

"Excellent. I did a little of that, as well." She popped her laptop off its dock and moved to sit beside him at the table. "Let's see how much overlap there is in what we found."

She angled her laptop so he could see her screen and scooted closer. He caught a whiff of something sweet and floral. Did she do it on purpose?

He glanced at her and their gazes locked.

She smiled.

Was that a hint of sadness in her eyes?

"Are you okay?" Why did he ask? He wasn't going to get involved with the Rick situation. Or at least, that was what he kept telling himself.

Stephanie looked away. "I will be. It just gets old."

"I'm sorry."

She glanced back and let out a mirthless laugh. "You don't even know what I'm talking about, do you? Because you probably were sitting here asking what I did to get Rick riled up in the first place."

Chris fought a wince. "If he missed a deadline, it had to be addressed."

"It's worse than that. He called the client—which he shouldn't be doing in the first place—and let them know that their contractual deadline was stupid, his word, and that he wouldn't be pushing to make it just because they'd thrown a dart at the calendar. Also his words."

"Eesh." Christopher frowned at his laptop monitor, unwilling to meet her gaze. "And you found out . . ."

"When the customer called me to see if they needed to have their lawyers involved." Stephanie shook her head. "So I'm scrambling to try to understand what happened while placating them with everything I have. Meanwhile, Danica let me know she's transferring over to Cyber because she doesn't want to work in a division where there's even the remotest possibility that she'll have to bail Rick out again. And then, I barely hang up with the client—having mostly repaired the damage, but not quite—and Rick comes blustering in because I had sent him an email letting him know that the deadline stood, he would make it, and to see me if he needed help."

"I'm sorry." There were no other words. He'd misread the situation—although he could still stand on the idea that raising her voice wasn't the right answer. But if Rick was escalating, it might have been necessary. Given the disrespect the man was showing when Chris turned up, maybe it was the only way to get through.

"It's fine. Hopefully HR can figure it all out now. Salil was getting in touch with Joe to give him the scoop. I don't imagine Joe is going to have a lot of tolerance for someone who jeopardizes contracts and longstanding client relationships."

"Ha. No. I'm guessing he won't." Christopher reached over and lightly touched her arm, letting his hand rest there for a moment before moving away. "I'm still sorry."

"Thanks. So." She pointed to her laptop screen. "Let's get to work. I'd like to get done in time to grab some dinner before prayer meeting."

"You're going tonight?" Christopher didn't usually go to the Wednesday night service. There were all kinds of classes in addition to the larger prayer and worship service, but with church Sunday and the Bible study on Monday, he was generally ready for a quiet night at home when Wednesday rolled around.

"I always try to make it. Why?"

"Want some company?" He didn't know who was more surprised by the question—her or him. But he wasn't going to bumble around and try to backtrack. She'd probably say no. Of course she was going to say no. There was no reason at all she'd want him to tag along.

"You know what? I really would."

STEPHANIE CRANED HER NECK, stretching to scan over the heads of the throngs in the church lobby. This was one of the problems of attending a megachurch—it was super hard to meet up with someone. Not that it had been a problem in the five-ish years she'd been coming here before today.

What on earth had possessed her to agree to meet up with Christopher for the Sunday service? They'd had a nice time together on Wednesday, true, but that had seemed perilously close to being a date. This probably tripped over the edge into that category.

It wasn't work related.

It was a prearranged time to do an activity together that would most likely end with them sharing a meal.

Maybe she'd been out of the dating world for a while, but it sure seemed like all the required elements were right there.

Something caught her eye. Just a flash of light brown hair and a distinctive gait. She concentrated harder on the crowd. Aha. There. She raised her arm and waved.

Christopher was scanning too—why did his thick, black glasses make her mouth water?—and there. He saw her.

He weaved through the crowd, his lips curving. "Good morning. I've never actually tried to find someone in the foyer before. I should've thought about that."

"Or I should have. It didn't even occur. But hey, here we are." Stephanie's stomach jittered with nerves. She moistened her lips. "Should we look for some seats?"

"Sure. You want to try the balcony?"

She shrugged. It wasn't her usual choice, but then, neither was sitting with someone she knew. "Why not?"

He grinned and gestured for her to go ahead of him.

She wormed through the crowd toward the double doors that led to the stairs. The throngs eased once they were climbing up to the balcony level, though it wasn't empty by any stretch of the imagination. Once upstairs, she stopped and waited.

"Would you believe I'm not sure where to go at this point?"

"You haven't sat up here before?" He chuckled. "I like it. I think the acoustics are better."

"Okay." Acoustics weren't really her concern. She just wanted to be at church and learn something about Jesus. Preferably something that would help her be more like Him in her own life. "So which doors?"

"Those straight ahead are the fireside rooms. The balcony entrance is right here." He reached out and grabbed a door, then pulled it open.

Ah. She'd seen announcements mention the fireside rooms for their meeting locations. Now she knew where they were if any of them were ever interesting enough to attend. "Thanks."

The balcony was filling up. Stephanie followed him to the

front row, where he found space on the pew that would accommodate both of them.

"This okay?" He glanced over before sitting.

"Yeah." Stephanie sat and looked out over the sanctuary below.

"What do you think?"

"It's nice. A new perspective is always a good thing."

Christopher turned and held her gaze as her heart gave two lazy thuds. "It is."

She didn't think he was still talking about the balcony. Was he starting to change his opinion about her? Stephanie swallowed. That would be nice. Not because she was interested in him—nothing like that—but it would sure make working together easier if he could admit she wasn't automatically the one at fault all the time.

All she could do was nod.

The choir filed in, filling the loft. The orchestra took their seats in the pit. Stephanie's eyebrows lifted. How had she not realized this was a traditional service? She usually came to an earlier one where the worship band led the music. This should be interesting.

The first strains of violins were quickly joined by more instruments and then the joyous voices of the choir. Stephanie sucked in a breath. How had she never tried this service before? The choir was phenomenal.

The words were still projected on the screens, but they weren't words she knew. *A mighty fortress is our God.* She'd heard that before somewhere, hadn't she? She looked around. People near them were singing. In fact, so was Christopher.

She glanced at him. He had a clear tenor, and it wasn't at all what she'd expected.

Well, to be fair, she hadn't really known what to expect.

At the end of the first song, the pastor invited them to pray. At least this was the same as she was used to.

It was distracting having Christopher beside her through the service. Warmth radiated from him, keeping Stephanie sharply aware of his presence. She was able to focus well enough to stand and sing, but when Pastor Brown began the sermon, it took every ounce of her concentration to follow along.

Finally, after what seemed like twice as long as a typical service, the pastor prayed the benediction and quiet music was drowned out by the sounds of people leaving.

"So? What'd you think?" Christopher picked up his Bible from beside him and stood.

Stephanie clicked her phone off and tucked it in her purse. "It was different, but I liked it. I'm glad I tried it."

"Yeah? Think you'd like to come another time?"

Stephanie pressed her lips together. What was he asking? "Maybe?"

"I wouldn't mind trying out the contemporary services again. They're not my thing—and yeah, I know, that's weird for someone in our generation, but I grew up with hymns and choirs, and I just love them."

"Music nerd." Stephanie grinned to soften her words. "Who knew the unplumbed depths of Christopher Ward?"

"Well, I did." He chuckled and tucked his hands in his pocket, his Bible held against his side by his elbow. "Is it weird if I invite you to lunch?"

"A month ago, yeah, it would've been. Now? I'm going to go with no. And I'd like that."

His whole face brightened. "Really? How do you feel about delis?"

"If there's a Reuben, I'm good."

"Best Reuben I've ever had." He drew an X over his heart

while he spoke. "Would you maybe want to ride with me? I can bring you back to your car when we're finished."

Stephanie swallowed. She didn't like riding in other people's cars. It was a nice offer—was she going to be considered a shrew if she said no?

"Or not. We can meet there. It was just a thought." He was backpedaling faster than she could think.

"Sorry. I have a thing—it's a long story. I could drive? Same deal. You'll have to navigate, obviously."

He studied her, then nodded. "All right. Sure."

Her shoulders relaxed. "I'm parked in the side lot."

"Yeah, I saw your Jeep and parked beside it." He grinned. "I was already thinking about lunch. I forgot breakfast."

"How do you forget to eat?" She shook her head as she started toward the exit. The crowd had thinned quickly—which made sense. The Sunday school classes and life groups all started in another five minutes. There was barely time to make it if the service ran over. It was one of the reasons she often used as an excuse not to get hooked into a smaller group. That and she just didn't want people prying into her life. It wasn't as if they'd actually care.

Christopher fell into step beside her once they were down the stairs and in the foyer. It was still crowded—that was a constant whichever service was coming up, it seemed.

Stephanie pushed open the door, stepping to the side to hold it for him.

"Thanks."

"Sure. So this deli, how'd you find it?"

"Ryan recommended it. Not sure how he found it. But honestly, most of the good places to eat I learned from Ry. He's a wannabe foodie."

Stephanie snorted out a laugh. "I would never have guessed that about him."

"How well do you know him?"

She shrugged and dug out her key fob. She clicked the Unlock button twice. "Door should be open."

When they were in, and buckled, she started the engine. "I've worked with him once or twice. Not enough to make assumptions, I guess. But the one lunch meeting I was in with him, he had some kind of weird cheese sandwich."

"Pimento cheese." Christopher shuddered. "Bet you a dollar. He makes his own. It's part of the foodie thing."

She wrinkled her nose. "I thought being a foodie meant you liked fancy, delicious food."

Christopher laughed. "Yeah. You'd think. With Ry? It mostly means he likes weird and unusual stuff. Some of it's great. But not everything. Turn left when you get to the light."

The deli wasn't far. She'd actually been to the shopping center where it was located a few times. There was a furniture store in there that had some fun imports.

Parking near the restaurant was full. She backed into a space that was a bit of a walk. "Are we going to be able to get a seat?"

"Should be. We might have to sit at the counter. That okay?"

Stephanie shrugged.

Christopher grinned and they hurried between parked cars. A crisp, cold breeze whipped across the lot.

It was definitely still January.

He grabbed the door and held it for her.

Heat surrounded her and she rubbed her hands together. "Brr."

He laughed before glancing at the hostess. "Two?"

"Counter okay? Or I can squeeze you in the back corner." The older woman snapped her gum and looked like she couldn't care less.

Stephanie looked around. Caricatures filled the walls—she

recognized some of the faces as local celebrities, but the others seemed to be normal people.

"What do you think? Table or counter?"

"We can try the table." The counter wouldn't really be conducive to talking—and in spite of herself, Stephanie was beginning to realize she enjoyed conversations with Chris.

"All right, let's give it a shot."

"Follow me." The hostess slid off the stool she'd been perched on behind the podium and started sliding between tables.

They were crammed in the space—did the fire marshal ever actually come and see about the occupancy in here? It seemed well over any reasonable limit.

In the far back corner, a table had been shoved into a corner and chairs were wedged against the two open sides. There was almost enough room to pull them out and sit without asking the people at the nearby tables to move. Almost.

"Maybe we should've done the counter." Christopher scooted his chair in another little bit and sucked in an exaggerated breath.

Stephanie chuckled and her knees bumped his. She ignored the tingles that raced up her leg. "No, this is better."

He shook his head. "You say."

She flipped open the menu, eyes widening at the columns of offerings. "How do you choose?"

"I don't. I get the Reuben."

"You've never tried anything else?"

"Nah. Ry swears by their club if you're more in the mood for that. But seriously, if you like a Reuben, you want that."

"All right." She flipped the menu closed and folded her hands on top of it. "Tomorrow's the one-month check-in with Tyler. What do you think that's going to be?"

"You really want to talk about work?"

Stephanie froze. It had seemed like a safe conversation to start. She wasn't the best at small talk. Or interpersonal relationships. Which was, of course, why everyone thought she was a horrible human being. "We don't have to. But you'll have to choose the topic."

"Okay." He leaned forward, his gaze steady on hers. "Tell me about your time in the Army."

Stephanie swallowed. Why would he want to know that?

6

Stephanie sipped her coffee and kept her head down. The conference room was loud and it grated on her nerves. Everything did this morning. She'd changed outfits three times before finally acknowledging she was going to just have to deal with everything seeming tight and itchy today. She hadn't slept much, and when she had, she'd dreamed.

They weren't nightmares anymore, at least. But they weren't the kind of dreams that got discussed over breakfast, either.

Not that she had anyone to discuss anything with over breakfast.

Which was fine. It was. She was fine. Everything was fine.

"Morning." Christopher was cheery as he pulled out the chair beside her at the conference table and sat. "How are you?"

"Fine." She sipped the coffee and wished she could leave it at that. Why couldn't people just leave her alone? But she needed to be nice. He was her teammate—and yesterday, before lunch at least, there'd been those brief glimpses that hinted at a possibility for more. That was gone, of course. It always disappeared when she talked about the Army. Stephanie sighed and forced a polite smile. "How are you?"

"Good. It's a new day. New month. Endless possibilities ahead."

She rolled her eyes.

"What?"

"Why doesn't it surprise me that you're an optimist?"

He laughed. "Why doesn't it surprise me that this annoys you?"

"Funny guy."

Christopher rested his fingers on her arm. "Seriously, are you okay? You look kind of rough."

"Gosh, way to turn a woman's head." She knew she was pale. Hadn't she layered on foundation with a trowel this morning trying to hide that? And she'd run out of concealer working on the circles under her eyes. All for nothing, it seemed.

"Sorry."

She glanced at him and sighed at the red staining his cheeks. "It's okay. I didn't sleep well. It happens. I'm sorry I snapped."

"Want to get coffee after the meeting?"

Stephanie wiggled her cup from side to side and the coffee sloshed. "Yeah, sure. I'll probably need a refill by then."

Chris patted her arm and removed his hand.

She shouldn't miss his touch.

"All right, everyone. Take a seat." Tyler rapped his knuckles on the table. "I'd like to keep this meeting short and sweet. So far, Joe and I are pleased with what we're seeing from the teams. After a little hiccup at the start with several of you."

Titters made their way around the room.

At least she and Chris hadn't been the only ones who had tried to avoid working together right out of the gate. That would've been bad. Very, very bad.

"Anyway. It's February first, and what's February known for?" Tyler paused.

Stephanie frowned. President's Day? Being short? What was he getting at?

"Oh, come on. Valentine's Day!" Tyler laughed. "Which you're probably now thinking has nothing to do with running a business, but you're wrong. Morale is a thing, and it's going to be the focus of our efforts this month. You need to prove that you're willing and able to keep the spirits of your team high—and keep them invested in working here. There are thousands of jobs in the Tyson's Corner area. More than that if you expand out into Arlington, Crystal City, D.C., Springfield. You get the idea. This area is crawling with opportunities to make a change if people are unhappy. Turnover is bad for business, but so are disgruntled employees. So, your mission, should you choose to accept it, is to figure out how you're going to get your employees to love their jobs so they aren't buffing up their résumés on their breaks. Questions?"

Stephanie bit her lip. This was a disaster. Christopher had reported her to Joe because she was challenged when it came to this kind of stuff. Ugh! At least this time he had to help her figure it out. But still.

"Yes, Melanie?" Tyler pointed across the table to the girl from the video game division who'd raised her hand.

"Does it have to be Valentine's Day themed?"

"No. We just want people to love working here. Love. Valentine's. Get it?" Tyler grinned. "Other questions? No? Great. Get to it. I'd like to see your proposals by the end of this week. You have the whole month to execute, but it's better to get those ideas in motion sooner rather than later."

Stephanie drained her coffee as Tyler stood and strode from the room. Several of the other teams were already leaning in and whispering to one another. They probably had so many ideas they were going to have to pick and choose. Gah. If Joe and Tyler had designed a challenge specifically to knock her out of the running, this was it.

She didn't care if people loved working here! She just wanted them to do the job, get paid, go home, and relax. Then come back the next day and do it again. That was what she did.

"You ready for that coffee?" Christopher touched her hand.

Darn tingles. What was with that? Of course, he was starting to get touchy-feely, so that might have something to do with it. "Yeah. Let's get out of here."

Stephanie pushed back her chair and stood. She grabbed her notebook—she hadn't written anything down. There'd been no need. This ridiculous assignment was going to be seared on her brain to feature in her nightmares for years to come. On the way out the door, she dropped her empty coffee cup into the trashcan before following Christopher to the elevators.

"Some challenge, huh?" He pushed the Down button and shoved his hands into his pockets.

"It's like they're targeting me. I don't know how to do this." She swallowed. That had come out more easily than she'd imagined it would. When had it gotten so easy to talk to him? She glanced over at him in time to see sympathy flash across his face.

"We're going to figure it out. It's not exactly my strong suit, either."

Stephanie snorted. "Oh, sure. That's why everyone loves you and thinks I'm a shrew."

His cheeks reddened. "That might be a little dramatic."

Right. She was a dramatic shrew. That was much better. She stepped into the elevator when it arrived and leaned against the back wall.

Christopher pressed the button for the ground floor. No one joined them before the doors closed. That was unusual, but she wasn't going to complain.

"So, want to walk down to the coffee shop at the corner?"

Christopher glanced over at her before returning his gaze to the large display showing what floor they were passing.

"Yeah, okay." It wasn't her usual haunt—she was fine with the break room coffee. But if he wanted a change of scene, she could go with it. Easygoing. That was her new motto, right?

The elevator arrived at the ground floor and the doors slid open. Christopher gestured for her to go first and followed close behind. Outside, Stephanie wished she'd thought to zip back to her office and grab her coat.

"Oh, wow. We don't have to go if you'd rather hit the lobby kiosk." Christopher rubbed his arms. "It's brisk."

Stephanie laughed. "That might win 'understatement of the year.' Just walk fast."

She strode down the block toward the coffee shop he'd mentioned. He jogged a few steps before falling into step beside her. "So, is this an Army thing?"

She frowned and glanced over. What was it with him and her service? "Is what an Army thing?"

"The long stride and fast pace."

"Sorry. I can slow down." It probably was left over from the military. The boots were heavy and tended to elongate strides. She'd gotten used to it. Plus, there was no room for dawdling in the Army.

"Nah. It's okay. I'm just curious. You don't like to talk about it, though."

"Not so much." She'd told him more at lunch yesterday than she'd shared with anyone in a long time. And look how well that had worked out. Too much more, and she'd be back in therapy. No, thank you. Not that there was anything wrong with it, she just could think of about six hundred things she'd rather do than spend an hour exploring her trauma every week. Better to leave it alone and not rock the boat.

Christopher nodded and reached for the coffee shop door.

"Sorry. I'll try to remember that. I think it's great, though, for the record."

"Thanks." She never knew what to do with that. It was nice —much better than people saying she was a bigot or murderer because she'd served overseas—and yet, to her it didn't seem like a big deal. The Army had put her through college, and she'd found she enjoyed the camaraderie and work then and when she'd gone full-time active duty. Until she'd been injured, and they'd decided she was too damaged to stay.

Too damaged. Story of her life.

She breathed in the rich coffee smell and moved toward the counter to order. "May I please have a large coconut latte?"

"Whipped cream?"

"Yes, please." Stephanie dug in her pocket for her wallet.

Christopher reached out and touched her hand. "Can I get it? Please?"

He'd paid for her lunch yesterday, too. She turned to study him. He looked so earnest. Hopeful. She nodded. "Okay. Thank you."

"My pleasure."

Stephanie shifted to the pickup area while he ordered and paid. What was this they were doing? Should she ask him? That was her usual choice when she didn't understand something— just barrel in and get it figured out. Everyone said that wasn't feminine. And it contributed to the perception of her as intimidating and brusque. She blew out a breath. Fine. She'd try to take it as it came.

"Coconut latte."

"That's me." Stephanie took the large cup and turned to study the tables. She nodded to a spot in the back corner, near a fireplace. "You want to sit over there?"

"Yeah, I'll be right there."

Stephanie crossed the mostly empty café and took the seat

that put her back in the corner. She sipped her coffee and closed her eyes as the sugar hit. Maybe enough of that plus caffeine would get her through the day.

She opened her eyes and watched Christopher as he headed her way. This sure felt like a date.

There was a part of her—a big one—that was okay with it being one.

CHRISTOPHER SETTLED across the table from Stephanie and sipped his mocha. The heat from the drink warmed him as it traveled down. After the chill walking from the office to here, it was a good thing. "So. Any thoughts on how we make people love working in government services?"

Stephanie shook her head. "I'm still struggling with why we care. Sure, there are a ton of other job opportunities out there. But if you flip it around, it means there are a ton of other people who we could hire if we needed to. And maybe they'd be a better fit overall. Take Rick."

"No thanks."

Stephanie laughed and pointed at him. "Exactly. Who hired him? It wasn't me. And I don't understand how he got through our screening process. He's incompetent, misogynistic, and a pain in the rear."

"Nothing from Salil yet about helping him move on?"

She shook her head. "I checked in this morning. He said it could be a week or two."

Chris frowned. That didn't seem right. Not after the clear problems Rick had been causing. "Okay, so we want to be sure Rick doesn't love it here."

She chuckled and sipped.

"Do you love it?"

She blinked. "Do I love working here? I mean, I guess. Do you?"

He nodded. No question. "This is the best job I've ever had. I love the flat management structure. I love the camaraderie. I love the fact that there's always someone who can help if I get stuck and that the work we do is meaningful and challenging."

"Okay, see? Those are good things to springboard off of." She flipped open the notebook she'd been carrying since the meeting and started to write. "How do we leverage those sorts of things into an event?"

"Would it be crazy to have a Valentine's Day social?"

Stephanie sent him a bland look. "Really? We're like eighty percent male. You realize that, right? It's not exactly the recipe for romance."

"Right." He rubbed the back of his neck. That wasn't what he had meant—not really. "I was thinking more the whole 'love your job' thing."

"Do people even want to love their jobs, though? Seriously, aren't most people content to get paid to work and then go home and relax?"

Was that all she wanted? Why had she even accepted the invitation to be part of this competition? "Does it matter? This is what Joe and Tyler want us to do."

She sighed. "True."

He bit his lower lip and spun the sleeve around his coffee cup. "Let's table that a second. Is that all you want? Just a job that you do, then go home?"

"Yes and no. I want to be appreciated for what I bring to the table. I'd like to know that what I do matters, but let's be real. Nothing I do in a software company is going to matter as much as what I did when I was deployed. So there's some scaling there, you know?"

"Okay. That makes sense. So what would it take for you to

love your job?" Maybe she'd come up with something they could work from.

"I guess knowing people weren't badmouthing me behind my back." She shrugged and sipped. "But I know I'm the office joke. Don't mess with Stephanie, she's a 'b' word."

He winced. She wasn't wrong. And he was responsible for some of that. "I'm sorry."

"It's fine. But you see what I mean, right? I'm not looking for my work to be some kind of fairytale where we dance through the cubes and whistle in harmony."

He chuckled. "I guess we'll scratch off team-building musicals then."

"Probably wise." Stephanie pinched the bridge of her nose. "I told you I wasn't going to be able to do this. Maybe I should bow out. You'd be better at this than me. People *like* you. Joe should just choose you and let it be."

"Hey." Christopher reached across the table and took her hand. "People like you."

"Yeah? Who?"

He squeezed her fingers. Their warmth traveled up his arm. "Me, for starters."

Stephanie looked away.

He touched her chin and swiveled her head back so he could meet her gaze. "I like you a lot. And maybe it was surprising at first, but that's on me, not you. I listened to the gossip and I had preconceptions that crumbled when I actually started working directly with you. You're smart and capable and exactly the kind of woman . . ."

Her eyebrows lifted. "Exactly the kind of woman?"

He took a long drink of coffee. Why didn't he stop himself before he'd gone there? Although, maybe it was better to lay it all out. "That I've been praying for my entire life."

"Oh."

He searched her face, but it was hard to read her thoughts. The "oh" hadn't been super encouraging. Should he say something else? Ask a question, maybe? "Are you okay?"

"Yeah. Just surprised, I guess?"

Was that a question he was supposed to answer? He didn't know if she was surprised or not—well, actually he could figure it out. She looked like he'd beaned her in the face with a pole. "Sorry."

"No. Don't be. I'd be lying if I said I hadn't been starting to lean in that direction myself. I just figured it was something I should get over on my own."

He grinned. "I'd rather you didn't get over it."

Pink stained her cheeks. "Okay. Um. I guess I'll try not to."

"That's a start." Hesitantly, he slid his hand across the table, palm up.

Swallowing, Stephanie put her hand in his. "We still probably have to figure out how to make people love their jobs."

He chuckled and closed his fingers around hers. "Yeah. That's true. But maybe I can concentrate on that a little more now that we have this out of the way."

"Was it in the way?" She looked up and met his gaze.

"Only from the standpoint that it was all I could think about." Christopher drained the last of his coffee. "We should probably get back to the office, though. Maybe we could get dinner Friday and then spend some time working on our plan?"

A smile bloomed on her face and she nodded. "That sounds good. Do you want to keep having our end-of-day meetings?"

"Are you kidding? Of course I do." He squeezed her fingers. "I want every opportunity to spend time with you. Can we do prayer meeting again on Wednesday, too?"

"I'd like that." Stephanie scooted her chair back and started to stand. "This wasn't how I expected getting coffee to go."

"Better, right?" He stood, still holding her hand, and sidled closer. The heat from her body warmed him. At the same time, it sent tingles zipping through him.

"Much better." She inched away, creating a little more space than he'd left.

It was something she did—Christopher had noticed it in other situations, too. He'd ask her about it another time. For now, it was enough that she seemed content to hold his hand. More would come with time.

He could wait.

What would this change in terms of the competition?

They still had to work together—even though they were technically competing. He frowned slightly as they left the coffee shop and headed into the fierce cold.

"It's still chilly." She hunched her shoulders and picked up the pace.

"It is." And he'd let her go on thinking it was the cold that had made him frown. A decision settled in his gut. They were competing, absolutely, but Stephanie would win. She deserved it. She was already higher on the management chain than him and, personality issues aside, she knew what she was doing.

Stephanie deserved to win.

And if he got to be with Stephanie, then he would win, too.

7

Christopher pushed the vacuum back and forth over the living room floor, a list of things to get finished before Stephanie arrived zipping through his brain.

"Bro." Ryan yelled over the noise and tapped on Christopher's shoulder.

He jolted and flipped the switch. "What?"

"What's going on? You got a hot date I don't know about?"

"Date? Please." Christopher forced himself to stop talking before he started babbling. Ryan was a big fan of reading into things. "What about you?"

"Me? Nah. Thought I might hit the gym again. It's becoming a Friday night thing for me, you know?" Ryan laughed. "Stephanie coming over to talk strategy?"

"Last time I talked to her, that was the plan." Christopher tried for a nonchalant shrug. "When do you and Jess find time to work on your stuff?"

"Here and there. I'll probably give her a call after I work out. But we've got a leg up on this morale thing—everyone loves working in cyber. You don't last long there if you don't."

Christopher snorted. Not so in government solutions. He still hadn't managed to come up with any ideas. "Don't you still need an event?"

"Oh, sure. But c'mon. How hard is that going to be, really? We just have to get all the folks who love their jobs already to do something together. Easy peasy."

"Well. Good for you." Christopher frowned. Was he over-thinking things? Was Stephanie? Even if they were, it didn't give him any ideas of what to suggest for their morale booster. He flipped the vacuum back on and got back to work.

Ryan shook his head before heading out.

When the condo was clean—or, well, cleaner, at least—Christopher stowed everything away and headed into the kitchen. Stephanie had talked him into carryout again—it made sense, since they did need to work on their plan—but he wanted to take her out somewhere nice. A real date. One where they didn't have to talk about work that was hanging over their heads.

They'd get there eventually.

At least Wednesday had been sort of like that. They'd gone to dinner at the deli before prayer meeting. But still they'd had their own cars and had come and gone separately. What would it take to get her to let him pick her up and take her out?

He filled a glass with ice and poured lemonade from the plastic pitcher in the fridge. Anything that he could do with his hands would be a good thing. Why was he nervous? It was just Stephanie. They'd been getting together every day at work and every Friday in the evening for a month. This was no different.

He snorted.

It was *so* different. This was their first official date. And it wasn't even a good one. Why had he let her talk him out of dinner out somewhere fancy? Or even casual. Something nicer than hanging out at his table like they were used to doing. The way this was going, they'd end up talking about work, too.

Ugh.

How lame could he get?

The knock on the door jolted him out of his spiraling self-doubt. He finished the last swallow of lemonade, set the glass in the sink, and headed to answer the door.

"Hi." Stephanie grinned.

"You look nice." He took a minute to appreciate the fancy slacks and boldly green sweater that peeked out of her unzipped jacket. He reached for the takeout bags. "Let me get those. Come in."

"Thanks. You look good, too."

He smiled and headed toward the kitchen to set down the bags. "I'm honestly surprised Ryan didn't say something to me about what I was wearing. He seemed a little preoccupied."

"Well, I'm glad." Stephanie shrugged out of her coat and looked around.

"Sorry, I'll go hang that up."

"Can I get out plates and stuff?"

"Sure. That'd be great." He carried her coat to the tiny closet near the front door that he and Ryan used primarily for sports equipment and cleaning supplies. They both tended to keep their coats in their own closets. One lonely wire coat hanger, only slightly twisted out of shape, dangled on the rod. Christopher frowned at it. Was that even going to hold her coat? With a shrug, he hung the garment then waited a moment to see if it was going to slide off. When it didn't, he shut the closet door and padded back to the kitchen.

"Almost all set." Stephanie looked up from dishing barbeque onto two plates. "When I saw this place was still running their smoker even though it's winter, I had to get it. It's a little house near mine—I think a couple generations of the family all live and work together. It's the best barbeque I've had since I was stationed in Georgia. Nobody beats real Southern barbeque, but this comes as close as you're going to get in Northern Virginia."

"That's . . . brave."

"What is?" She picked up her plate and started toward the dining table.

Christopher got his own and followed. "Eating food out of a pop-up kind of place like that. What about the health department and all that?"

Her eyebrows lifted and she shook her head. "I guess it's a risk, but when you've eaten meals brought to you by locals who you *think* are supportive of you being in their country, but you're not completely sure? Mom and Pop barbeque isn't really a blip on the radar. Besides which, they very proudly display their inspection certificates in the front window. Probably for people like you who are going to be looking for them."

Heat washed across his face. He cleared his throat. "What can I get you to drink? We have powdered lemonade, assorted sodas—even diet—or water."

"You bought diet soda?"

Christopher nodded.

"I'll have that. Thanks."

"No problem." He darted back into the kitchen and grabbed two cans of soda from the fridge. He set the diet in front of Stephanie, then sat at the spot next to hers and reached for her hand. "Do you want to say grace?"

"Okay." She bowed her head and was quiet a moment before thanking God for the food and for their time together. It was short and simple, but it warmed him all the way through.

He squeezed her fingers before removing his hand from hers. "I don't want to talk about work all night, but I did have a bit of an idea that I wanted to mention. Maybe it's worth exploring, or maybe it's dumb."

"Stop that. Tell me what it is. It's not going to be any dumber than some of the ideas I've had."

Christopher sliced off a bite of brisket and popped it in his mouth. He closed his eyes as he chewed.

"Told you."

"Shh. This is a moment."

Stephanie laughed. "When you're done with your moment, tell me the idea."

"Okay, here it is." He paused and sipped his soda. "What if we talked to Joe about having a happy hour at his place in Georgetown?"

"Hmm." Stephanie focused her gaze on her plate as she sliced her brisket into precise squares. Finished, she set her knife down and tented her fingers. "I kinda like it. Do you think he'd go for it?"

"I don't know. That's the big 'if.' I was thinking a regular happy hour might be a reasonable second-place idea. There are certainly some nice places near the office we could all get together at. But Joe's might make it more about loving the company. And if we footed the bill for catering, all he'd have to do is let us in. Or maybe we could look into renting those stand heaters and have it in the garden—depending on when. You know how the weather gets in February. Some days, it's straight up spring."

"I like the idea of outside, but we'd have to be sure about the weather. I feel like I heard something about him having an actual ballroom in that place though. So if he'd let us use that, we wouldn't be tromping through his whole house. We should put together a solid justification for holding it there as part of the pitch. It'd sure stretch the budget they gave us."

"Maybe, maybe not. Parking in Georgetown is a pain, so we might need to consider renting a shuttle. That plus catering is going to easily eat the budget. Which means maybe a nearby restaurant where we could walk is a better idea."

Stephanie stabbed two of the brisket squares and popped them into her mouth. She chewed thoughtfully, then nodded. "Why don't we both think on it this weekend—maybe work up the pitch for Joe and proposals for both options, then we can compare notes on Monday and, if we can get on his schedule, try to see Joe either late Monday afternoon or early on Tuesday."

That was a reasonable suggestion. At least she hadn't shot down the idea. A happy hour wasn't completely original—but having it at Joe's would be special. A reminder to everyone of who started the company, who remained at the helm, and everything he stood for. "I like that. And maybe, if it goes over well, we could look at having a regularly scheduled happy hour closer to the office every other month or something."

"I like that. Plans to continue to bolster morale. But we're not making it mandatory, right?"

"Nah. That takes the fun out of it. And of course that means maybe we're missing the people who need a little *esprit de corps*, but forcing them to come wouldn't get them that, either."

Stephanie laughed. "No. It really wouldn't."

He grinned and took another bite.

They chatted about a variety of non-work topics for the rest of the meal. Stephanie helped him load the dishes into the dishwasher and clean up the food containers. She ran the kitchen sponge over the countertops, rinsed it, and set it beside the faucet before turning and cocking her head to the side. "What do you want to do now?"

"Movie? Board game?" This was the problem with having stayed in. He didn't have a ton of options beyond that to suggest. Not that if they'd been out, he wouldn't have offered the movie option—it just would've been in the theater.

"What sort of movies do you like?" Stephanie asked.

"No old Westerns, I prefer no one bursts randomly into song, and explosions are a bonus."

Stephanie laughed. "You're such a guy."

"Guilty." Christopher offered his hand and tugged her closer when she took it. "Why don't we go see what we have on hand? And there are all the streaming options, too. I'm sure we can find something that'll work for both of us."

"Probably so. I poke fun, but I'm also not a big fan of Westerns or musicals." She sat on the floor beside him in the living room so they could look over his DVD collection.

He only invested in the actual disc when he was a big fan of the movie, so the options were semi-limited. Ryan had a slightly larger collection, but he kept them in a binder in his bedroom. Ry never minded when Christopher borrowed a movie, but he hadn't wanted to ask. It would lead to too many questions, and neither he nor Stephanie were ready to go public with their relationship just yet. There was nothing wrong or against company policy with them dating—she'd checked—but it was new, special. And they'd both agreed it would be nice to keep it that way, at least for a little bit.

"I like this one. And this one." Stephanie tipped two movies out.

"They're both winners. Lots of good explosions. You choose."

She reached for the one featuring a reboot of a spy thriller series by a popular author from the '80s. "This one. It has a little romance, too."

So it did.

Christopher took the DVD case, opened it, popped out the disc, and slipped it into the slot on the Xbox. "Do we need popcorn or anything?"

"I'm stuffed." Stephanie stood and crossed the room to the couch. She settled on an end, tucking her legs under herself. "Are feet okay? I should've asked."

"Please. This couch belongs to two guys. It's had worse than feet."

She snickered.

Christopher sat beside her, careful not to crowd her space. He hit the power on the TV remote, then used the Xbox controller to get the movie started. He glanced over at her and extended his arm along the back of the couch.

Stephanie looked up, smiled, and shifted so she was leaning against him, her feet tucked the other way.

He laid his cheek on top of her head and curved his hand around her shoulder as the opening action began. He wanted to kiss her.

It was too soon.

He'd remind himself of that as much as he had to. For now, he would just enjoy the sensation of having her in his arms.

STEPHANIE BRUSHED at the sides of her skirt as the elevator rose to the top floor. She and Christopher hadn't managed to get in to see Joe yesterday, but he'd made time for them this morning. And since he was the owner of the company, they'd both dressed up more than usual.

But she should have worn a pantsuit.

She had plenty of those and they didn't make her crazy like skirts did.

Of course, the sparkle of admiration in Christopher's eyes when he'd first seen her might have made it feel a little more worthwhile. Did it offset the whole wearing-a-skirt thing? She wasn't sure. Probably not.

The elevator dinged and the doors slid open.

"Here we go." Christopher glanced over at her with a bolstering smile.

"The worst he can say is no. We have a backup plan. A solid one. This would be better, but it's not the end of the world." She clamped her lips shut when he frowned at her. "Sorry."

"No. It's okay. Just . . . try to be positive?"

"Right. Positive." That was *so* not her natural inclination.

Stephanie forced a smile for Joe's admin. "Good morning. Stephanie Collins and Christopher Ward. We have an appointment."

"Go right on in, he's expecting you." The admin smiled before she turned back to her computer.

Christopher gestured for Stephanie to go in. Which, okay, chivalry, et cetera. But really, she didn't like being the first through the door when it felt like there might be a firing squad on the other side. And that was unreasonable. Sort of. Unless she focused on the fact that the only time prior to now when she'd dealt with Joe one-on-one, it was to be reprimanded for not being friendlier. Because Christopher had complained about her.

Water under the bridge. Had to be. He didn't feel that way anymore, anyway.

Stephanie strode confidently into Joe's expansive office.

Joe stood from behind his desk, his smile warm. Friendly, even. "Good morning. You're right on time. Have a seat at the table and I'll join you. Do you want coffee?"

"No thank you." Stephanie slipped around the table to a seat that would keep her back to the wall. Old habits were hard to shake.

Christopher took the seat beside her. He patted her leg under the table.

The mix of sensations was distracting. It was probably intended to be friendly—but there was no such thing as casual contact when it came to Christopher. Even the tiniest brush set off fireworks under her skin.

She cleared her throat as Joe settled across the table from them. "Thank you for squeezing us in. We won't take long. Um." She flicked a glance at Christopher and he nodded at her. Right. She'd just keep going. "We're working together on the challenge for the government services arm."

"And? How is that?" Joe leaned forward, his arms resting on the table.

"Good, I think." Stephanie looked at Christopher, eyebrows lifted.

"Definitely good." He grinned at her before turning back to Joe. "Getting to know Stephanie has been eye opening. In a good way. She's fabulous at her job and an absolute asset to the division."

Heat washed across her cheeks. "I feel the same way about Christopher."

Joe grinned and leaned back. "I'm glad to hear it. I'll admit to having a slight hesitation about putting the two of you together after the fall. It's good that you've settled your differences and found a way to make a strong team."

"And friendship, too." Christopher smiled at her. "No one's more surprised by that than I am."

"Well, I might be." She waited while Joe laughed, then continued. "So the love-your-job challenge kind of threw us at first. And we spent a lot of time brainstorming, finally landing on the idea of having a happy hour."

Joe frowned slightly. "That doesn't seem like it should have taken very long to come up with."

"Well, no." Nerves churned in Stephanie's stomach. "Our twist, at least the twist that we'd like to talk to you about, is having it at your home in Georgetown."

"Hmm." Joe pressed his palms together and bounced his fingers against his mouth. "Why?"

"Well, for one thing, it's your continued involvement in the company—even after the division takes place—that sets Robinson Enterprises apart. You're the head and the heart. Government contracting jobs are a dime a dozen in this area— we don't really have a unique product that gives us a specific edge. But we have you. And you've done a lot to distinguish how we do what we do from other local companies." Stephanie paused and wished desperately for a drink of water to soothe her desert-dry throat.

Christopher slid his hand across the table so it barely brushed hers. He reached for the portfolio in front of her and flipped it open, then took the top page and offered it to Joe. "We did a quick survey yesterday, asking as many of the division as we could track down what it was that kept them here. Most of the answers boiled down to you. So I think—we think—it's important for us to show that a change in leadership doesn't mean they're losing anything. That you're still going to be there."

One corner of Joe's mouth poked up as he scanned the document.

What did it mean? He hadn't said no outright, but he also hadn't jumped at the idea. Then again, Stephanie wouldn't be rushing to volunteer her house either. She couldn't blame him. But she still very much wanted him to say yes.

He looked up, nodding slowly. "You've made a good case here. I'm open to the idea. I need to check the dates to be sure we're in town. What would you need from me or my staff?"

"Nothing." Stephanie took another sheet out of the portfolio and offered it. "Your budget for the event was generous and we think it should easily cover cleaning and catering. We didn't want to inconvenience you if you were going to open your home. You just have to show up and smile, have a drink, and maybe eat something."

"I think I can do all of that." He ran a finger over the sheet of paper. "I appreciate that you made public transportation mandatory. Parking is tricky and I don't have the space for more than ten or fifteen cars in my parking area. There are options for valet that we could have explored, but this also means that if someone opts for alcohol, there's no chance of them driving afterward."

"No, sir. That was something we were adamant about." Stephanie looked over at Christopher, who nodded in agreement. "We discussed making it all non-alcoholic, but the reality is, that would keep several people from coming. As it is, we're thinking everyone gets one drink ticket. Soda, tea, and coffee are unlimited. In fact, one caterer I spoke to said they could set up a fancy coffee bar, so it'd be a little more interesting than just black coffee and single serving creamers. There would be a barista and some fun options."

"I like that. You've put good thought into this. I'll get back to you by the end of the day, but I don't foresee any problems. Good thinking, you two." Joe pushed his chair back and started to stand.

Stephanie collected her portfolio and stood. "Thank you. So much. I know it's a lot to ask of you to open your home, but I think it'll end up being meaningful. To everyone."

Joe extended his hand.

Stephanie shook it. Christopher followed suit.

It was hard to keep from babbling, but they were clearly dismissed. Joe was on his way back to his desk and Christopher had started toward the door. Stephanie lengthened her stride, hoping it didn't look like she'd lagged behind.

As they passed Joe's admin, a grin split her face. She nudged Christopher with her elbow.

He looked over, also grinning. "That went well."

"It really did." She pushed the Down elevator button. The doors slid open immediately and they stepped inside.

Christopher pushed the button for their floor and, when the doors closed, tugged her into his arms. "Good job."

Stephanie laughed and relaxed against him. "I'm glad he went for it."

"Me, too." He held her close, his eyes searching hers. After a moment, he inched his head closer.

She drew in a quick breath, her eyes drifting closed.

The elevator chimed and the doors began to open.

Stephanie jolted and dashed to the corner, hugging her portfolio to her chest. The doors opened all the way and a chattering group came on. From their ripped jeans and graphic T-shirts, they looked like they were programmers in the video game arm of Robinson Enterprises.

"Nah, man. There has to be some advancement in XP after you take down a mid-level, or people will riot."

One of the guy's compatriots jammed his elbow into the speaker's ribs.

"What?" He looked around and appeared to see Stephanie and Christopher for the first time. "Oh. Sorry. You know how it is."

"Sure." She offered a small smile. The elevator finished descending to their floor and chimed. "Excuse me."

Stephanie slipped around the knot of game programmers and stepped out. Christopher was directly behind her, frowning slightly.

"That . . ." He reached for her hand.

Stephanie glanced around quickly before grabbing his fingers and giving them a fast squeeze. "It's okay. Maybe you'd like to get dinner tonight after work?"

"I'd like that. A lot."

"It's a date." She winked, her insides warming at his words. "I should get busy. There's a lot on my plate today."

"Yeah. Me, too. Tonight though, right?"

She nodded, smiling. It was confirmation for dinner, certainly, but also a promise to finish what he'd tried to start in the elevator.

Or at least she hoped so.

She pressed a hand to her quivering belly as she strode down the hall to her office. If kissing Christopher was even close to what she imagined it would be, it was going to be a very pleasant evening.

8

Stephanie's gaze flicked to the clock in the corner of her monitor. Almost time, but ugh! It was like every minute went slower than the one before.

Should she have a suggestion of where to eat ready? It had been her idea, after all. Did that mean she should pay? That was fine, she didn't mind. But maybe he would want to? Or they could split it. That was never a bad thing, either.

She closed her eyes and fought the urge to cradle her head in her hands. This was why she didn't date. Well, this and the fact that it was unusual for someone to be interested enough to ask her out. Let alone try to kiss her in an elevator at the office.

A knock on the door jolted her out of her circling thoughts. "Come in."

Rick pushed open the door and scowled at her. "You went to HR."

Stephanie didn't sigh. There was no point. In fact, it had taken longer than she'd expected. "I did."

Rick swore at her. "You're out to get me just because I can prove you're bad at your job."

"I'm sorry you feel that way. Why don't we call Salil and have this conversation with him on the phone?" She hit the Speaker button on her desk phone and quickly entered the HR rep's extension. "Go ahead and pull a chair up."

Rick crossed his arms. "I'll stand."

"This is Salil."

"Hi, it's Stephanie Collins. Rick's here with me."

"Oh?" The sound of shuffling papers floated through the phone's speaker. "Hi, Rick. What brings you to Stephanie's office today?"

"You can't do this to me. The two of you are conspiring against me—you're probably sleeping together. I'll sue both of you." Rick's voice rose with each word and he ended the sentence screaming.

"Rick." Stephanie frowned at him and shook her head. She pointed to a chair and motioned for him to sit. "Salil, do you have all his paperwork there?"

"I do. It's all in order."

"Paperwork? What paperwork?" Rick threw himself into the chair in front of Stephanie's desk, scowling.

Salil's voice came through the speaker loud and clear. "The paperwork you've signed during your tenure here. We have performance reviews with clearly outlined steps for necessary improvement. Signed. We have follow-ups when those steps were not completed satisfactorily and a new action plan, also signed. Then there are the complaints."

Rick snorted. "Like anything this woman wrote up matters."

"Well, actually it does. She's your boss. But she isn't the only one who filed formal complaints against you for abusive language, sexual harassment, and making a hostile work environment." Salil cleared his throat. "Should I go on?"

Rick glowered but kept his mouth shut.

Stephanie frowned. How had he managed to stay employed so long with those sorts of complaints? She'd be asking about that when Rick wasn't around, that was for sure. It was one thing when she thought it was just a problem with her. But this? It couldn't be allowed to continue.

"Very good. We'd planned to have this conversation on Friday, but seeing as how you decided to cause another problem today, I think it's best that we handle it now. Stephanie?"

"Rick, you're fired."

"But—"

"I'll escort you to your desk to collect your personal items. Salil, could you have someone from security meet us there?"

"Of course."

"The security officer will escort you from the building. I hope you know better than to use me as a reference, but I will verify your employment if asked." Had she left anything out? She'd only skimmed the email Salil had sent, thinking she had until Friday before she had to deal with this. "Do you have any questions?"

He shook his head, still scowling.

"I'll meet you at Rick's desk. There's a little bit of paperwork that will need to be signed. Give me about five minutes." Salil said before the phone clicked.

Stephanie pressed the Speaker button to hang up and rose. "Come on. Let's go gather your things."

He stood and crossed his arms. "You can't do this."

Stephanie offered a tight smile and gestured for him to precede her out of her office. There was no point in arguing. Salil would bring the termination paperwork and a security officer, and Rick would be out of her hair once and for all.

"Stephanie." Christopher called out as she and Rick started down the hall. He jogged the last few steps to catch up. "Hey, Rick."

"Ward. Maybe you can fix this. Certain people," Rick shot a

glare at Stephanie, "seem to think they have the authority to fire me."

"Which I do. And it has happened." Stephanie gritted her teeth. Why couldn't Christopher have been just a little late? "I'm sorry, I'm going to need about thirty minutes before I'm ready to go."

"Sure." Christopher tucked his hands in his pockets. "Okay if I tag along?"

It really wasn't. She didn't want him here—she could handle this. On the flip side, maybe having another man there would keep Rick in line. Because apparently external plumbing somehow conveyed authority. "If you want, and if it's okay with Rick. Salil's meeting us at his cube."

"Yeah, come along. Pretty sure you can help me cut through whatever bamboozle this chick has worked on the HR dude." Rick's pouty stomp turned into a strut.

Stephanie shook her head. The man was delusional. "The paperwork is done, Rick. You're going to sign it, pack up, and then someone from security will escort you from the building."

"Is that necessary?" Christopher reached out and touched her arm. "He's not a criminal. That seems excessive."

"It's procedure." Stephanie's jaw clamped down around the words. Was he really questioning her in front of the guy? Seriously? "As I'm sure you're aware?"

"Well, okay, it's in the book, but come on. This is Rick. He can be a jerk, I get that, but he's got a family."

Stephanie stopped, turning to face Christopher. Her blood was at a near boil. She took a deep breath. Then another. Screaming was not the right thing. A third deep breath and her heart rate settled back to just slightly elevated. "Maybe you could wait for me in my office? Thirty minutes. Tops."

His eyebrows lifted but he held up his hands and took a few backward steps. "All right. Don't rush on my account."

Stephanie nodded and watched as he turned to stride down the hallway. That could have gone better. Christopher would probably spin it so it was her fault—everyone tended to—but she wasn't in the wrong here. She caught up to Rick at his cube.

Salil and a security guard were already there.

Rick was loading picture frames and knickknacks into a box. "This is dumb. I'm not signing anything. I'm going to sue you all for wrongful termination and then we'll see who ends up in charge of this company. Maybe I'll go after Robinson and win the whole shooting match. Then you'll all be out on your ears, and I'll be the one laughing behind my hand."

"No one is laughing about this, Rick."

Salil shot Stephanie a sharp look and shook his head. "You will need to sign the papers. It's a simple acknowledgment that you've received them and we've gone over everything they entail. If you feel you have a case for a lawsuit, a signature on these papers won't change anything. Failure to sign them isn't going to change your termination, but it will impact how we respond to any employment verification inquiries."

Stephanie fought to keep her lips from twitching. Now she almost wished he wouldn't sign, then she'd be able to lay out in clear and precise details all the ways Rick was unfit to hold a job anywhere.

Rick must have thought it through, because he seemed to freeze for a ten count before angrily reaching into the box for a pen. He snatched the papers from Salil and scrawled his name on the last page.

"You need to initial here." Salil flipped a few pages and pointed to a shorter line. Rick scribbled. "And also here."

"There. Happy?" He bared his teeth at Stephanie in what was probably supposed to be a grin.

She forced herself not to react.

"I believe that pen is company property." Salil pointed as

Rick tossed the writing implement back into his box. "In this case, I suppose we can let it slide."

Rick crossed his arms. "Seriously? I can't take my supplies?"

"Did you bring them from home?"

"No. That's why there's a cabinet in the break room."

Salil shook his head. "Then no. Those supplies are provided for employees to use to carry out their work on behalf of the company."

"Then I guess I'm done." Rick tipped his box so Stephanie and Salil could see its contents. Aside from the pen, they were all his personal belongings.

Stephanie nodded to Salil.

"Great. Then please come this way, Rick. I've got it from here, Stephanie."

"Thanks." She swallowed. She didn't want it to come to this. There had been remediation plans in place that Rick had blown off. She'd tried to find a place to transfer him where he could have a male supervisor and a job that he was capable of completing. None of it had worked. It wasn't her fault—but it sure didn't feel that way.

When the little group turned the corner and disappeared from view, a handful of people who were still working clapped.

Stephanie winced. That was why it had to happen. But it still didn't feel good. She turned and headed back to her office.

Christopher was kicked back in her guest chair doing something on his phone. He glanced up as she came through the door and offered a hesitant smile. "Ready to go?"

The low-grade throbbing behind her left eye that had started when Rick barged into her office was gradually increasing. Her stomach was unsettled. It may have been what she needed to do, but she hadn't enjoyed it. And now? If she went to dinner as planned with Christopher, he was going to want to talk about Rick—and all the ways that she'd failed to do the job properly so the man could stay employed. There was no way kissing was on the menu tonight. Not now.

"I am. But I actually think I'm going to head home."

Christopher frowned as he stood and tucked his phone in his pocket. "Are you okay?"

She shook her head.

"Are we okay?"

She glanced up and met his steady, earnest gaze. "I don't know. What are we doing? You don't even like me. You never have."

"I do like you. A lot. I'll admit that I did not, initially, understand you—but that's changed now that we've spent so much time together." He reached for her hand, but let his arm drop back to his side when she didn't take it.

"Okay." She didn't think he was telling the truth. Not when he was so quickly willing to jump in and defend Rick, questioning her responsibility to let the man go right in front of everyone. But she also didn't want to fight about it. Not right now.

Maybe not ever.

What would be the point?

He sighed. "Can I at least walk down to your car with you?"

Stephanie shrugged. She shut down her laptop and loaded it, along with some files, into her bag. She grabbed her purse, checked that the file drawer was locked, and started toward the door. "If you want."

"I do. I don't want there to be a problem between us."

"Okay."

"That's it?"

"I don't know what else to say, Christopher. I don't have the energy to fight with you right now."

"I don't want to fight with you." Concern filled his expression and he stroked her cheek. "I want to take you someplace nice for dinner and spend an evening not talking about work."

She smiled slightly as she opened her office door and started into the hall. "Rain check, okay? I just need to go home."

Christopher studied her, his lips pressed together. Finally, he nodded. "Tomorrow?"

"Maybe. We'll see, okay?"

He sighed and followed her into the elevator.

Stephanie leaned against the back wall and closed her eyes. She couldn't take him looking at her like that. He was hurt. So was she.

Maybe the distance between them was too great to cross after all.

CHRISTOPHER KICKED the condo door closed behind himself and dumped his things on the floor. He toed off his shoes and left them beside the pile. Between Stephanie shutting him out and traffic deciding to suck, he was in a foul mood.

He stomped to the kitchen and yanked open the fridge. Maybe dinner would soothe some of the jagged edges. Hangry was a thing. He stared at the nearly barren shelves. When was the last time someone had gone to the market? Was it his turn or Ryan's?

"Ry?" No answer. Christopher shut the fridge and wandered through the condo. Empty. Which was strange. Because Ryan had said he didn't have plans tonight. Christopher had hooked his hopes on a night relaxing with his best friend. Maybe he was just running late.

Pizza sounded good.

He slipped his phone from his pocket and dropped onto the couch as he navigated to the app for their favorite delivery place.

Laughter echoed down the outer hallway, growing louder as whoever was entirely too jolly for their own good got closer to the condo. *Just keep on going by. Take that madness off to someone who can share it.* He tapped a favorite order, checked the tip percentage, and confirmed the pizza.

A key grated in the lock and the door opened, revealing his sister hanging on Ryan's arm, giggling. And the way Ryan was looking at Jess had Christopher flying to his feet.

"What's going on here?" He scowled at them, arms crossed.

"What are you doing home?" Ryan shifted away from Jess and gestured for her to go through the door.

Jess's shoulders fell but her face held a bright smile. "We were going to work on our love-your-job event. Ryan thought you were taking Stephanie out. Big date, right?"

Christopher frowned at his sister as she made exaggerated fluttery eyes and kissy lips at him.

Ryan snorted out a laugh that he quickly turned into a cough. "I'm going to check the fridge. But we might have to order in."

"So. No big date, I take it?" Jess crossed the room and rubbed Chris's arm. "What happened?"

"I don't want to talk about that. What's going on with you and Ryan?"

"We're working on a project together, remember? Duh." She rolled her eyes. "Come on, Chris."

"That's not what it looked like." He could feel his scowl deepening, even as he tried to stop it. "You were hanging on him."

"He told a funny joke. Sue me." She cocked her head to the side. "I'm a grown-up, you know. I could actually date someone if I wanted to."

Sure. Someone. Not Ryan, though. Not her brother's very

best friend in the whole world. "I acknowledge the theoretical possibility."

"Thanks, *Dad*." She shook her head. "If you were treating Stephanie this way, it's no wonder she bailed on your date."

"I didn't do anything wrong."

"Uh-huh. Sure."

"I didn't." He threw his arms in the air. "All I did was ask a question."

"What was the question?"

He made an exasperated growl in the back of his throat. "She fired Rick. And okay, the guy can be a jerk."

"Can be? Give me two for-instances when the dude wasn't a jerk." Jess pointed a finger at him. "Tell me you didn't try to advocate for him. He should've been gone a long time ago."

"You don't even work with him. How would you know?"

Jess shook her head. "Sidestepping the question is an answer in the affirmative."

"No, it isn't. And you didn't answer my question, either."

Jess laughed and perched on the edge of the coffee table. "Sit down before you have a stroke. I know because, as a woman, I've been warned about him. He'd get handsy in the elevators. He was always making off-color comments about women then trying to play it off as joking around when we'd get offended. And everyone in the entire company, I imagine, knows he never did his work. He goofed around until someone had to pick up his slack. The guy should've been gone before he was hired."

Okay, maybe she had some points. Christopher had heard the gossip—but he didn't like to form his opinions based on hearsay. The Bible was pretty clear about not participating in that kind of stuff. He fought a wince—it hadn't stopped him when it came to Stephanie. But he'd changed that. Didn't that count for something? "Did he hit on you?"

"Me? Nah. I wear jeans and graphic tees most days. That's

not going to catch his eye. Plus, I'm not high enough on the food chain to bother. Or I hadn't been. Since the contest, I've been taking the stairs to be sure I avoid him." She shrugged. "It's good to get up and move around, anyway. Elevators make you lazy."

He scrubbed his hands over his face.

Jess was watching him with a sympathetic smile. "You goofed up big, didn't you?"

"I guess. I still stand by the fact that all I did was ask a question."

"Did you call her authority into question with this inquiry? And was it in public or private?" She waited a beat, then nodded. "Yeah. That's a deep hole you dug yourself, bro."

"She has a reputation, too, you know. And I've seen it in action. Personally."

Jess closed her eyes. "Please tell me you didn't bring that up."

Had he? Christopher scrolled through the conversation, such as it was. "I don't think so."

"Which means you probably did. Or she at least knew you were thinking it. Good luck mending that fence. What'd she say when you tried to pick up and go on your date like nothing had happened?"

"That she was too tired to fight with me tonight but she'd take a rain check." He rubbed the back of his neck. "Was that her letting me down easy?"

"I guess you'll have to wait and see." Jess reached out and rubbed his arm. "But hey, at least you've got me and Ry. Let's order pizza."

"It's already on the way." Christopher's head dropped back against the couch and he shut his eyes. "You should go tell Ry so he doesn't try to come up with soup made from ketchup or something equally inedible."

Jess chuckled.

He felt her brush past his knees and heard murmurs in the

kitchen. This had been a seriously lousy day. How much crow was he going to have to eat to fix things with Stephanie?

Was she worth it? Yes.

Of course she was.

Wasn't she?

9

Christopher swung by Stephanie's office around lunch. Maybe he could entice her to take a little walk. There was a Peruvian chicken place that wasn't too far of a walk, and the yucca fries were amazing. His mouth watered. Maybe he'd go on his own if she turned him down.

Please don't let her turn me down, Jesus.

He needed to apologize. That was step one. But after that it was all going to be up to her. They couldn't fix this if she wouldn't talk to him.

He really wanted her to talk to him.

Christopher knocked on her closed door and waited, listening. He frowned when there was no answer and leaned closer. Maybe she was on a call and hadn't heard or couldn't answer? But it was quiet. He tapped again and tried the knob then eased the door open a crack so he could peek in.

The office was dark. She wasn't here.

He frowned. Where would she have gone?

He pushed the door all the way open and took a few steps in to study her desk. Her laptop was gone from its dock. If he had to guess, she hadn't come in today at all.

Now what?

Back in the hallway, he made sure her office door was shut and leaned against the wall. After a minute, he pulled his phone out and sent a text.

Hey. Stopped by to see about lunch. You're not here?

Would she respond, though? That was the real question. If she was angry enough to skip a day of work—or work from home—she was probably too angry to text. Or, maybe, this wasn't about him at all. That was a possibility.

Maybe not a realistic one, but a guy had to let himself hope, didn't he?

His phone dinged and he blew out a breath as he unlocked it.

Sorry no. Bad migraine last night. Working from home.

Ugh. Sorry to hear that. Can I bring you dinner after work?

The three little dots danced, indicating that she was typing. They stopped but no message appeared. Then they were back. They stopped and started several times before finally:

No, but thanks. Still going to try to make church. I'll grab something after.

Can I meet you there?

It was a long time before the next text appeared.

If that's what you want.

How was he supposed to answer that? Of course it was what he wanted. He wouldn't have asked if it wasn't. Maybe it was better to let his actions speak for themselves. He'd just go and find her at church after work. And then he'd make sure he was invited to share a meal with her, too. They needed to talk this through like adults.

People didn't throw away the chance at a solid relationship because of a misunderstanding. And okay, maybe he'd been obnoxious. He could fix that. He'd apologize. She'd forgive him, wouldn't she?

He was going to spend the rest of the day praying she would.

The chicken wasn't as appealing without Stephanie to share it with. Christopher detoured by the vending machines on his way back to his office. Maybe a candy bar and soda weren't the most mature choice, but who trusted sandwiches in a machine? Not him, that was for sure. At least he knew the Snickers wouldn't have gone bad.

The afternoon didn't exactly fly by, but it was busy enough to keep him from staring at the clock for more than two or three minutes at a time. He and Stephanie exchanged several emails about the catering and invitation details for their happy hour at Joe's place downtown. The invites needed to go out today so people had a little over a week to get back to them about attending.

Everyone would come, wouldn't they?

A chance to see inside Joe's Georgetown mansion would get him into a cab or onto the Metro without even a second thought. And they'd settled on Thursday, rather than Friday, so people didn't have to give up date night.

Date night.

Was that ever going to happen with him and Stephanie? Or had he blown it?

The thing was, even though Jess had been clear about where he'd gone wrong, Christopher wasn't sure he saw it that way. Stephanie had issues with speaking too bluntly and not giving people grace. She'd admit to that. So wasn't it okay for him, as a friend—possibly more than a friend—and fellow believer to point that out and challenge her on it?

And fine, he should have pulled her aside, not asked in front of Rick. He would definitely own that. But had he really been wrong? He just wasn't sure. Last time they'd butted heads over her personality and how it influenced her management style, he'd gone to Joe about it. He wouldn't do that this time. But surely she could see that he wasn't the only one at fault here?

His sister's litany of stories about Rick flitted through his mind. If even half of it was true, firing him had been the right thing. But Christopher hadn't seen it. Or, well, okay, he'd seen a little of it that day in Stephanie's office. But people had bad days all the time.

He pinched the bridge of his nose and checked the clock. Close enough. He wasn't getting work done, anyway. He'd pack up and head home. He could hit the gym and have a shower before prayer meeting and maybe between those two activities, he'd figure out the way to approach the conversation they needed to have that didn't end in her deciding she wanted nothing more to do with him.

Because despite all of this, he missed her. One day without hearing her voice and getting even a few minutes with her and he was miserable.

Was that a good thing or a bad one?

Only time would tell.

STEPHANIE CHOSE a pew near the front of the sanctuary and slid to the middle. She'd arrived early so she could get this spot because it was about as far from their usual seats as she could get. The balcony wasn't open for prayer meeting—they just didn't have that many people who came. But she and Chris had been frequenting the back three or four pews, depending on when they arrived, so it was likely he'd look for her there.

Was she hiding?

That didn't seem super mature. Ugh. And yet, the idea of the conversation that they needed to have set her stomach twisting into knots. It wasn't that she couldn't handle confrontation—she honestly didn't mind that—but this was more important, somehow. Which meant if she messed it up, the stakes were higher.

And messing things up was definitely something she was good at.

She covered her face with her hands and tried to pray.

Someone tapped her shoulder lightly. "Are you all right?"

At least it wasn't Christopher. She lowered her hands and fought a wince. It might not be Christopher, but Pastor Brown wasn't really any better. "Yeah. Sort of."

He smiled. Crinkles formed at the corners of his eyes. His hair was graying at the temples, but that was the only outward sign of the many years he'd been the pastor here. "'Sort of' isn't a ringing endorsement."

She laughed and it ended as a sigh. "Yeah. Relationships are confusing."

"Aren't they just?" He settled back and checked the watch on his wrist. "You don't have to, of course, but there are about fifteen minutes before everyone rushes in with five minutes to spare. I've been told I'm a good listener."

Stephanie bit her lip. She probably wouldn't have ever sought out the pastor for something like this. But he was here. And she'd been praying for help, so, maybe this was God's way of answering her prayers. She took a deep breath and let the story spill out. Her hands balled into fists as she spoke. "And so now I don't know what to do."

Pastor Brown's smile was kind. "It sounds like you do. You need to explain all that to him, the same way you did me. Not the facts, since it seems he knows that, but how it made you feel."

"He should know that, too. Shouldn't he?"

"Maybe. There are a lot of things in this world men should know that we seem to miss." His eyes danced with laughter. "Just ask my wife. The thing is, he probably felt he was being helpful."

"By undermining my authority and questioning my judgment and ability to follow procedure?"

The pastor wobbled his hand from side to side. "By pointing out another side of the situation."

She sighed. "One that assumes I have to be wrong, because I have a history of not always acting kindly in the moment."

Pastor Brown laughed. "I think we all have that history."

"Not the way I do."

He shook his head. "I would imagine he wasn't setting out to hurt you. He was just doing the same thing he accused you of doing: speaking without thinking."

That was true. She could mention that when they talked. "Is it wrong that I want the person I'm involved with to support me? To think the best of me until it's proven otherwise?"

"Not at all. That's what love does—it says so in 1 Corinthians. Love hopes all things, believes all things." The pastor tilted his head to the side. "He hurt your heart, not just your ego."

She closed her eyes and nodded. Stephanie would have liked to say it was just her heart, but that wouldn't have been true. Her ego was definitely at play, too. "And maybe there's a little conviction in there, as well, because I wasn't sad to see Rick go. I didn't enjoy firing him, but I definitely enjoyed that he was fired. If that makes sense?"

"Of course it does. And it's not right to revel in the downfall of others—even others who we feel deserve it. Because what do any of us deserve except eternal punishment?"

She nodded. Stephanie had experienced a lot of grace in her life—not just from Jesus, but from others. She needed to do better at living a life that extended that grace to the people around her. "I did try—a lot—with Rick. He had second and third and fourth chances. At some point, doesn't it have to run out?"

"God brings and allows consequences into our lives, even though we're forgiven of our sin. I think we just need to make sure we aren't the ones looking for reasons and ways to punish the people who annoy us. 'Vengeance is mine, I will repay,' saith the Lord." Pastor Brown winked. "It's another hard one. Sometimes revenge feels like it would be pretty satisfying. But it never is in the long term."

"No." She sighed. She'd seen enough revenge in her time in the military to know firsthand that any satisfaction from that was temporary. "No, it's not. Thank you."

"My pleasure. I'm glad I saw you were here early. It kept me from second-guessing the subject of my devotional."

She started to laugh, then saw he was serious. "Really?"

"Every time. I may have a vocation that requires public speaking, but it's not a natural talent. God and I have had some words over the years about His decision to call me into ministry. But so far, He's kept me here. So He gets me through it."

"You do more than get through, Pastor Brown. I tried a lot of churches when I moved here. You are a consistent beacon of light and hope in Jesus, and I'm grateful for you."

He smiled and stood. "Well, thank you. That's always nice to hear. I'm glad I saw you sitting here. I'll be praying that things work out."

Stephanie murmured thanks as the pastor slid out of the pew. Was Christopher just looking at it from another perspective? Maybe. It still hurt, though, that he was willing to believe good things about Rick before believing the best about her.

Quiet chatter began to filter into her thoughts. She checked the time and got out her phone, then navigated to her Bible app and the notes app she used. At least that was becoming more common—more accepted. She'd been an early adopter of electronic notes and spent a lot of years getting the side-eye for being on her phone during church. She couldn't say she'd never been tempted to switch over and check an incoming email or text because of it, but it didn't happen often. And it meant she was never without her Bible and notes, so if she had a thought, she could scroll back through and refresh her memory.

"Is this seat taken?"

Stephanie glanced up and her heart lurched. Christopher looked so serious and uncertain. "No. Go ahead."

"I'm sorry." He lowered to the pew and angled so his knees bumped hers and he could meet her gaze.

She nodded. "Maybe we can talk at dinner."

"I'd like that." He shifted and settled in beside her. "How's your head?"

"Better. Thanks." She looked over and smiled. Maybe she'd judged him too harshly. And yet, her heart was still stinging. Because she needed someone who could love her as she was, not as some person she might eventually change into.

Pastor Brown walked down the aisle, stopping here and there to talk and shake a hand. When he passed by them, he quirked a brow and nodded at Christopher.

Stephanie smiled and dipped her chin slightly.

Christopher leaned close and whispered in her ear, "What was that?"

"Tell you later." She had to fight off the urge to giggle. Her cheeks burned.

On the stage, Pastor Brown nodded to the pianist and the opening strains of an older worship chorus began. The screens on either side of the sanctuary showed the words. Stephanie pushed away thoughts about the day and focused on singing.

Prayer meeting was less of a production than Sunday morning. It had a quieter, more intimate feel—starting with the music and continuing through the short devotional Pastor Brown gave, sometimes sitting on the edge of the stage instead of standing behind his podium, and the time spent in small groups composed of the people nearby praying down a printed sheet of requests.

This was what community should feel like. What church should be.

When it finished, and the pianist started playing quiet music, Stephanie reached for her purse.

"Where did you want to go to dinner?" Christopher stood and offered his hand.

She took it, lacing her fingers through his. The idea of sitting in a restaurant and having the conversation they needed to have wasn't something she really wanted. No one else needed to overhear—which left out his condo, too. Ryan had to be getting tired of excusing himself all the time.

Stephanie took a deep breath. "What if we grabbed takeout and went to my place?"

His eyebrows lifted. "Really?"

She nodded. She could trust him—she needed to trust him —at least she wanted to. If nothing else, it would give them the privacy they needed to hash things out.

"Okay. That still leaves the question of what kind of food." He started out the pew and down the aisle.

Stephanie followed, still holding his hand. "We could just grab burgers."

He wrinkled his nose.

"Or not." She chuckled. "You choose. I'm fine with whatever."

"You're sure?"

"Yeah. Here." In the foyer, Stephanie tugged her hand free of his and dug in her purse for her phone. She tapped out her address and texted it to him. "It's not far. I'll meet you there?"

"That works." Christopher checked his phone before he started walking again.

"I have water and sodas at home, if you don't mind diet. Otherwise get yourself something to drink, too."

He laughed. "Got it. I'll see you in maybe thirty?"

"Okay." Stephanie lifted one hand in a wave and headed into the parking lot. Christopher didn't follow—had he parked somewhere else? Maybe he was looking at the map to see what sort of food was on the way. It didn't matter—it gave her a chance to get home and . . . well, it gave her a chance to get home, anyway. She kept a tidy place—the Army would do that for you—and she'd worn jeans and a sweater to church, so it wasn't as if she needed to change.

Her house wasn't far. Stephanie opted to zip onto the Beltway for the two exits rather than winding around the back way. It wouldn't do for her to hit all the lights and end up with Christopher beating her there. She pulled her Jeep into the carport and hopped out, checking that she'd locked the vehicle before unlocking the door that led into the kitchen. She stopped and flipped the deadbolt when she was inside. He'd come to the front door, wouldn't he?

She put her shoes away in her bedroom, trading them for the slippers she tended to wear around the house. Then she started pacing. She walked to the front door, paused to peek out and check for his car, then straight back to the sliders that made the back wall of the house and faced the fenced yard. There were trees along the back fence line, providing privacy, and a small concrete patio just off the house. Then it was grass. One of these days, she was going to do something more interesting with the landscaping. She continued along the glass doors, then turned and made her way back to the front door before starting the process all over again.

She'd made seven circuits by the time headlights turned into her driveway.

Stephanie pressed a hand to her quivering belly and unlocked the front door.

10

"Were you waiting long?" Christopher strode quickly up the flagstone path to her front door and squeezed past her. "Wow. It's gorgeous."

She turned and looked at her house, trying to see it like he did. She couldn't quite get there. It was a nice house—built in the 1960s like all of the houses in her neighborhood. There was a little foyer, where they were standing, the kitchen was off to the right, the living and dining room straight ahead, and stairs led up and down on the left. Up to bedrooms, down to the space she used as her home gym. "Thanks. Come on into the kitchen. I usually eat in there."

"Okay." He followed where she pointed.

Stephanie shut and locked the door before going after him. "Have any trouble finding it?"

"Nope. I actually looked at houses in this neighborhood a year or two ago. Ryan and I were talking about investing together. This is walking distance to the Dunn Loring Metro, which is a big selling point." He opened the brown paper bag that had been tucked into a plastic one, and the unmistakable scent of Chinese wafted out. "Hope this is okay."

"As long as you got egg rolls."

He grinned and reached back in to pull out a crinkly packet. "Always."

Stephanie moved to the fridge and got out her bottle of soy sauce. "Soda or water?"

"Let's live dangerously and have soda."

She laughed and collected two cans while she was in there. Why couldn't it always be this easy and fun with him? "Here. Plates or containers?"

"Hmm. Let's go plates. Then we can share."

"Fair enough." Stephanie set her soda can on the table and went to gather plates and silverware—might as well go the rest of the way toward civilized. "It smells good. Which place did you hit?"

Christopher said a name and described the little shopping center where it was.

"I might have seen it. Don't think I've tried it, though. So this should be fun." She sat and waited for him to do the same.

"Let's pray first." He reached for her hand and said a blessing over the food and their time together.

Stephanie added her own silent plea for God to give her the words she needed to explain without hurting him.

When he finished, Christopher smiled and flipped open the containers of food. "I was out of line on Tuesday. I should have at least pulled you aside to ask my questions so Rick didn't hear. I'm sorry."

"Thank you." Stephanie took a container of rice and scooped some onto her plate. Was he not going to apologize for the content of the questions? She waited. But no, he seemed to be done. Awesome. She put the rice down and reached for what looked like beef with broccoli. "I guess I want to make sure you know you really hurt me. Not because you asked in front of Rick, although I didn't love that, but because you felt like you had to ask at all."

"What do you mean?" Chris furrowed his brow and paused in the act of adding rice to his plate.

"Do you feel like you have to protect people from me?"

"What? No. Of course not."

She kept her gaze steady on him. "Because it feels like that's what you were doing. Like you were saying there was no possible way Rick could have earned his dismissal aside from me being some kind of vindictive monster who was persecuting him and finally took it too far."

He looked down at his plate. "That isn't what I thought—or meant—at all."

"Then why would you defend him without knowing the whole story? Why wouldn't you defend me?"

"You can handle yourself."

She nodded and took a bite. "You're right. I can. Rick can't?"

"No. That's not—look, I already apologized for stepping in."

"No, you didn't. You apologized for doing it in public."

He sighed. "It's the same thing."

"It really isn't." Stephanie stopped herself and forced a deep breath. She took a bite and chewed as she weighed her next words. "Last time you didn't like the way I was handling things, you went to Joe to complain about me."

Chris's face turned a deep red. He gave a curt nod.

"Would you have had less of a problem with Rick being fired if a man had done it?"

He frowned. "I don't understand the question."

Stephanie pushed away from the table and paced to the fridge. "This is who I am, Christopher. I'm smart and I'm direct and while I'm working on tempering the directness so it doesn't come across as brusque and rude, the reality is that it may never change all that much. Because sometimes in this industry, you have to be direct and forceful."

"I just don't agree. You can catch more flies with honey."

"Oh, for crying out loud. I don't want to catch flies. I want people to do their jobs. I want clients to get what they're paying us for and *only* what they're paying us for. And I go about it the same way the other PMs do. The only problem that seems to exist is that I'm a woman, so therefore when I do it, I'm being a word that starts with B." Why couldn't he see it? Rick had been shuffled from contract to contract—department to department. No one had had the guts to just fire the guy, even though that was what needed to happen.

"I'm sorry you feel that way."

She put her hands on her hips and stared at him.

"What? Why don't you come sit down, okay? Your food is getting cold."

With a little huff of breath, she came back and sat. "You don't think I have a point at all, do you?"

"I just think maybe you're very sensitive to the fact that you're a woman."

Her eyebrows lifted.

"And I guess I don't understand what's wrong with being a little less direct if you get the same result."

"Let me ask you this, if you were so on fire for Rick to have a job, why didn't you let him transfer to one of your projects?"

He winced. "Because I would have had four of my best programmers—and yes, they're women—transferring out. I know he was a problem. I just think you could have handled it better."

"I see. And that would have been, what, ignoring the fact that I had people who refused to work with him also? Telling them to suck it up? What's your magical solution?"

"There are procedures in place. Remediation plans, mentors, all of that."

"You don't think I did that?"

"You did?"

"Yeah. I did. Twice, because I didn't want anyone to think I wasn't giving him the benefit of the doubt. He got more consideration than he should have." She forked up a huge bite and stuffed it in her mouth to keep from saying anything else.

"Oh." He sighed, his shoulders slumping. "Look, I'm sorry. For all of it—for making you feel like I didn't support you, questioning you, the whole thing. Can we please move past it?"

Stephanie opened her soda and took a long drink. Tears burned the backs of her eyes, but she wasn't going to let them fall. Not yet. He'd probably think they were angry tears, anyway, but why risk it? She swallowed. "Yes. Professionally, we can move past it."

"And personally?"

She shook her head. "I don't think that's smart. We got carried away in the moment—lots of time together, all of that, but I think it's pretty clear we're not a good match. You don't respect me—you don't even really like me—and I'm not so desperate that I'm going to try to settle for that. I'm okay on my own. And you're better off finding someone who fits your mental image of a Godly woman."

"Steph—"

"Please don't. This is hard for me, too. But it's better to call it now while we can still be friendly and continue working together." She nodded to his food. "Go ahead and keep eating. You can fill me in on your conversations with the caterers."

∼

"WHAT'S WRONG WITH YOU?" Ryan used the remote to pause the show on the TV as Christopher trudged into the living room.

He shook his head. It wasn't that he didn't want to talk about it—it was more that there was just no point. Stephanie hadn't let him make his case at all. Once she'd determined they were better off ending things on a personal level, she'd been all business.

Now what was he supposed to do?

"Sit down, man. I'll get the chips and salsa."

Christopher laughed. "I don't think chips are going to sit well right now. I had Chinese. It's not doing so great on its own."

"Nah, man. Chips make everything better. You know this. Sit. I'll be back." Ryan hopped off the couch and disappeared into the kitchen.

Christopher sighed and sank onto the end of the couch. Maybe chips wouldn't hurt. Maybe if he ate enough of them, he'd be too ill to go into work tomorrow—or for the rest of his life.

"So. You were hitting prayer meeting and dinner with Stephanie which, with my amazing powers of deduction, I am guessing did not go well." Ryan set a bowl of salsa on the coffee table and dropped an open bag of tortilla chips beside it. "What happened?"

"We broke up." He had to swallow the bile that rose as he said the words. Saying them out loud made them all too real. "She said I don't respect her. That I don't trust her. And that I should find someone who was a better fit for my vision of a Godly woman. Something like that."

Ryan dug into the bag of chips and came out with a handful. "And?"

"What do you mean, 'and'? Then she switched to professional mode and we talked about the happy hour while we finished dinner, and I left."

"You didn't fight for her?" Ryan shook his head. "Bro. Women always want you to fight for them."

"Not this one." Chris leaned forward and took a chip, dunked it in salsa, and crunched into it.

"So what, she says all that and you shrug, say okay, and leave?" Ryan frowned. "Do you respect, trust, and want her in your life that way?"

"Yes! Of course, I do."

"I don't think there's an 'of course' in this equation. You have to prove it."

"Yeah, well, she won't let me. She cut me off and made it clear that she'd said her piece, and we were done. I *respected* her enough to let it stand at that." Chris almost regretted the sarcasm that dripped off his words, but not quite. What did Ryan know? The dude hadn't had a girlfriend since college. "It's fine. I'll be fine. We still have to work together for this dumb contest, so it was better to agree and keep the peace and walk away."

"You really think the contest is dumb?"

"Yes. No. I don't know, man. Do I want the position, the responsibility, the possibilities of getting to direct the course of the company? Yeah. Of course, I do. But what's the cost? Because without the contest, I don't know if I would've been so aware of her behavior, and maybe I wouldn't have gotten into it with her about Rick—who totally didn't deserve my defense in the first place. So maybe we could've had a chance if not for that."

"The problem with that is that without the contest, the two of you wouldn't have been spending all this time together in the first place." Ryan scooped up salsa. "Right?"

"I guess." They had interacted off and on over the last couple of years. In fact, it had been increasing some over the more recent months. And then the contest. Well, then it was daily. He sighed. "I don't know what to do. Or that there's any point in trying. She seems pretty determined that we are back to colleagues. Period."

Ryan frowned and dunked another chip. "Valentine's Day on Sunday."

"Just no."

"What? Big, romantic gesture? Women love that."

Christopher shook his head. "I can almost guarantee that Stephanie does not fall into that camp. She isn't one who likes surprises. She sits with her back to a wall whenever she can, even if it means she's trapped in a corner. And you can tell she doesn't love being in that corner. Plus, I already apologized. The outcome of that little exercise? She dumped me."

Ryan snorted.

"I'm glad I can entertain you." He pushed to his feet. "I'm going to bed."

"Sorry. I'll be praying you find a solution."

"Thanks." Didn't seem like there was a point to that, if Christopher was honest with himself. He'd been praying about his relationship with Stephanie—asking for guidance and clarity. Well, he had clarity now, that was for sure. Seemed to him, this was God closing the door where something with Stephanie was concerned. So he'd keep working with her, do his best to perform well enough for Joe to choose him, and then . . . something.

He locked his bedroom door—something he didn't always do, but Ryan was probably going to try and check on him, and Christopher wasn't in the mood. He'd said his piece, and now it was time to move on. Get over it.

He dumped his work clothes on his overflowing hamper—he really needed to do laundry—and turned on the shower. He stood under the blistering hot water until it started to cool, got out, dried off, and put on his pajamas.

After climbing into bed, he dragged his laptop over. He

could work. There were definitely things to do. He sighed and opened a browser. He wasn't in the mood to work. There had to be a movie that would hold his attention until his mind quieted enough that he could sleep.

Preferably without dreaming of Stephanie and everything he had lost when she walked out of his life without a backward glance.

11

"You look nice." Stephanie started to reach out, then let her arms drop to her sides.

Christopher tried to smile, but it felt flat. "Thanks. You, too."

"It seemed like the way to go, since this was our event." She turned and looked out over the ballroom that took up the top floor of Joe Robinson's Georgetown mansion.

Christopher watched her wistfully before dragging his gaze away to look over the arrangements. They'd left work early to help the caterers set up. And now? It was good to go. If their department came and didn't feel a little happier about their jobs, then there wasn't anything he could do about it. "We did a good job."

"Yeah. We did." Her smile didn't reach her eyes. "I kind of hope whatever they have planned for us next month is easier."

"For sure." He tugged at his tie. They had four more months of this contest. Four more months where he was supposed to spend all his time working with Stephanie on whatever tasks Joe and Tyler assigned. Four more months of misery. Because the last week had been misery, so it seemed unlikely that it was going to get better. She was coolly professional and kept him firmly at arm's length. Any time he tried to veer the conversation toward something personal, she dragged it back to the topic at hand. Or ended the meeting.

He sighed.

"Hey, buck up. This is going to be a big win. One of the other groups sent their employees a valentine last Friday. Just a paper heart with a snack-sized candy bar stapled to it. Bo-ring." She chuckled. "Plus, I have to wonder what they did with the budget. Because paper and candy cost what, twenty bucks?"

Christopher shrugged. He wasn't going to worry about what the other teams did. What did it matter, really? "I guess the point is whether or not it made the employees love their workplace more. Maybe this is all overkill, and people will be annoyed that we cajoled them into coming."

Stephanie whirled on him, eyes wide. "You don't really think that, do you?"

"I don't know. It's Thursday night and we've asked them to come to a work event. Is it just one more obligation away from their family?" He rubbed the back of his neck. "I still think a chance to hang at Joe's—especially in the ballroom—isn't something I'd miss. But I'm single and don't really have much of a life."

Stephanie's mouth opened then snapped shut.

"Don't worry about it. Joe liked the idea. I'm sure it'll be fine." Christopher backpedaled. No need to panic her.

She shook her head. "I'm going to make another circuit and double-check everything one last time. You want to come?"

"No, that's fine. I'll hang out here and be ready to greet people as they arrive." He watched her walk off and fought the urge to rub his aching heart. Was this ever going to get easier? It wasn't as if he'd never dated before. He had. Seriously, even. Once. But that heartbreak was nothing compared to this. It made no sense. He and Stephanie had barely gotten together before she called things off. They hadn't even kissed.

He shook his head. He needed to get in the game. People would show up any minute now. He wanted them to love their job, not think the man who was potentially going to be in charge was cracking under the pressure.

"Looks amazing." Joe came to his side and slapped Christopher on the shoulder. "I should have more parties. I always think about it, but then I get into the planning and remember that I don't enjoy dealing with caterers and invitations and all of that."

Christopher chuckled. "It wasn't so bad, though I guess I wouldn't want to do it a lot. You could always hire someone. Or maybe your wife will want to?"

Joe laughed. "She's busier than I am—or she will be, once the contest is over. Cardiologists don't get a lot of downtime."

"True." What was he supposed to say to that? "Will she be joining us?"

"Not tonight. She's disappointed, but she had a work thing of her own." Joe smiled. "This got me out of having to attend. Did I thank you?"

"You didn't want to go?"

"Oh, I'm sure it would've been fine, but it's black tie. I much prefer business casual given the option."

Christopher laughed. "Glad to help. We really appreciate your willingness to host us here."

"It's a good idea. For them and for you."

"For me?"

"Sure. I can't promise the winners will end up billionaires, but multi-millionaire is definitely on the table when you look at compensation and stock options. So it's good to take a look at what that lifestyle might entail."

Christopher shook his head. "I don't imagine my lifestyle

will change that much. No offense, but a place like this for just me? There's no point. I'm happy in my condo for now. I'd like to get married, start a family—and that would mean a single-family home somewhere in the burbs, but nothing like this."

"Any prospects on the marriage front?" Joe nodded toward Stephanie, who was making her way toward them. "Maybe someone you've been working closely with?"

"I was hoping, but no." Christopher cleared his throat as Stephanie joined them. "Everything set?"

"Yes. Thanks, Joe. Really."

Joe smiled at Stephanie and patted her hand. "I was just telling Christopher that it was my pleasure."

"I think I hear the first group of guests." Christopher poked his head out the door, nodding as he spotted a group climbing the stairs. "We're on."

"You'll do fine." Joe gave a firm nod. "I'd like to continue that other conversation sometime soon. I'll have my admin get in touch."

Stephanie's eyebrows lifted as Joe wandered deeper into the ballroom. "What conversation?"

Christopher shook his head. "Nothing work related."

At least, he didn't think it was work related.

Nor did he think Joe was going to have any insight that would help Christopher fix things with Stephanie.

That ship had sailed. And it had taken his heart with it.

STEPHANIE'S FEET were killing her. She managed a smile, though it felt more like she was gritting her teeth than anything else, and offered the caterer their check. "Thanks again. You did an amazing job."

"You're welcome. Let us know any time you have catering

needs. You have my card?" The woman—what was her name? Paige, maybe?—dug into the pocket of her black slacks and pulled out a small, silver case.

"I think so, but I'd love another." Stephanie took the card and glanced at it. She did a mental fist pump. Paige Trent, owner and executive chef at Season's Bounty. "Thanks. You're top of the list next time I need to cater an event."

"Come by the restaurant sometime, too." Paige grinned. "Appetizer on the house. Hang on, let me put a note on the back of the card. It's a great place for dinner with your special someone."

Stephanie winced as Paige glanced between her and Christopher. "Oh, well, we aren't—"

"Or friends. I just thought—it doesn't matter what I thought. Although, if it matters at all, I think the two of you make a great couple. You're the easiest team-who-is-not-in-a-relationship I've ever worked with. And you look cute together."

"Thanks." Stephanie's cheeks were burning. She had to fight to keep from glancing over at Christopher. She cleared her throat. "You've got everything?"

"Oh, sure. We're good to go. Have a great night." Paige waved and started down the stairs.

"I think that was a success."

Stephanie jolted as Joe appeared, seemingly out of thin air.

He chuckled. "Sorry. I took the elevator. Well done. Both of you. Tyler was impressed, too. He said something about the sign of a good party was having to convince people you were serious about the end time."

Christopher grinned. "It took a little to get people heading out, didn't it? I'll go do one final pass of the ballroom. The cleaners should be done in thirty. Do you want me to wait?"

Joe shook his head. "I've got it. As long as they're paid."

"They are. I paid online yesterday." Stephanie chewed her lip. "I think one of us—"

"Don't be silly. Go home. You've got to be exhausted." Joe offered Stephanie his hand.

She took it. "Thanks. I'll go wait for an Uber outside."

She wanted to take her shoes off and hobble down the stairs, but that wouldn't exactly leave Joe with the right impression. And she didn't want to give Christopher the satisfaction. She gave in to the urge to sigh. She'd watched him all night when he wasn't looking. It hadn't been hard—it didn't seem like he ever looked over her way.

Did he care that they weren't together at all?

Why did she care if he cared? Ugh. *Don't be stupid, Stephanie.* She'd broken things off. And it had been the right decision. She couldn't be with someone who didn't see anything wrong with undermining her like that. Except . . . he hadn't. Not really. And he'd admitted his fault and apologized. But that didn't mean he wouldn't do it again.

Of course, there was no way to know if he'd do it again if she wasn't going to let him be part of her life. It was better to be safe than sorry.

Wasn't it?

She got to the front doors and turned, looking back up the stairs. Christopher hadn't started down—or if he had, he was taking his sweet time about it. Probably he and Joe were up there continuing the private conversation they'd been having before she'd arrived.

She frowned and pulled out her phone to order a ride.

It was fine. They could talk about whatever they wanted. She didn't have to be part of it. It didn't necessarily mean they were talking about her.

Oh who was she kidding? Of course they were talking about her. Christopher was probably explaining all her bad habits to

Joe to get himself a leg up in the competition. That was just like him.

Well, no it wasn't. Sure, he'd gone over her head to Joe in the fall, but when she tried to look at it objectively—and granted, that was hard—she could kind of see why. He *had* tried to talk to her first. She'd just blown him off.

A few minutes later, her phone buzzed. Stephanie checked the screen. Great, her car was here. That saved her from any more interaction with Christopher tonight. Or Joe. And she could take her shoes off in the back seat if she was stealthy. People said it was bad form, but her feet didn't stink and she really couldn't deal with the heels any longer.

She opened the door and hurried outside. She glanced back at the screen to confirm the color and car type before reaching for the door handle. "For Stephanie?"

"That's me." The driver nodded. He had music up kind of loud. She'd just take it as a signal that he wasn't chatty. That worked for her.

Stephanie climbed in the back seat, shut the door, and fastened her seatbelt. As the driver pulled away from the curb, she slipped her feet out of her shoes and curled her toes, barely managing to avoid a quiet "ahhh."

She let her mind go over the evening. Everyone had seemed to enjoy themselves. The food from Season's Bounty had been an enormous hit. She had to give Christopher props for that choice. Apparently, Paige's husband used to attend Pastor Brown's church? Or they still did? It was hard to keep it straight in her head—and she still hated the reality that in a church as big as hers, it would be impossible for her to recognize everyone who attended. Probably impossible even if she limited it to people who attended the same service she did.

Which actually brought up another sticky issue. What was she going to do about church? She'd enjoyed going with

Christopher. A lot. And church wasn't supposed to be about being with friends, but at the same time, it *was* about fellowship.

Hanging out with him had been the first time Stephanie had experienced fellowship in . . . forever. Since the Army, really.

She'd missed him at prayer meeting last night.

It made sense that he hadn't come. But still.

She'd made a huge mistake.

Stephanie closed her eyes as the realization hit, then spread through her like fire.

She swallowed the bile that tried to rise up her throat.

What did she do now?

12

Stephanie took what was becoming her usual spot at the first Monday of the month meetings with Tyler. The other eight teams seemed more subdued than usual today. Or maybe she was projecting. The last two weeks of working with Christopher had been strained and oh-so-polite. It made her teeth hurt.

She wanted things to go back to normal, but she just didn't know how to make that happen. She'd tried, unsuccessfully, to broach the topic a couple of times. He'd deflected. It was fair, she'd done it to him when they'd been eating Chinese at her house. And after. But gosh, it hurt more than she realized.

Did he not miss her at all?

He must not.

He wouldn't even sit beside her.

She shifted in her chair so she could look down the table to where he sat beside his sister and his roommate. The other guys in the room were all part of his Bible study, too. She needed to remember that. When it came to connections and networking, Christopher had her beat. Hands down.

No one in here talked to her. In fact, it was as if they

studiously avoided making eye contact. Because, apparently, she was just that horrible of a person.

This was dumb. She'd go up to Joe's office after this and back out of the contest.

Her stomach clenched.

Was she really going to do that? She risked another glance at Christopher and had to blink back the tears that sprang into her eyes.

Yes. That's what she'd do. Clear the field.

In fact, hadn't she said there were thousands of comparable jobs in the area when she was trying to understand why anyone cared if the employees loved their job? She would resign all the way. She had enough of a nest egg that she could work her two weeks' notice and spend a few weeks job hunting if she needed to. It was unlikely that it would take more than those two weeks to find something else.

Stephanie took a deep, steadying breath.

She wouldn't say she felt lighter—she didn't—but she was resolved. Having a plan was always preferable to waffling. There was nothing for her here anymore.

Not without Christopher.

It was her own fault. But she could fix it.

Moving on would have to fix it.

"All right everyone, let's get started." Tyler sat at the head of the conference table and rested his hands on the stack of folders in front of him. "This month, we'll be scheduling a couple of one-on-one check-ins as well as team-by-team check-ins. We know how we think things are going, but we'd like to hear from you what you think. So that's going to be the major task for you for the first two weeks of March—self-evaluation. We'll send out a rubric to guide your thoughts. Be honest."

There were quiet murmurs around the table.

Stephanie's lips twitched. It would be super tempting to try the interview trick of making sure that any faults came across as positives in disguise. Thankfully, she wasn't going to have to worry about it. Probably.

Maybe she'd have to do some of that to help Christopher succeed. But then, he was better suited for this all around, so he probably didn't need her help anyway. Well, she'd offer. He could say no.

"Other than that, Joe wanted to be sure you all knew he was impressed with the various activities that were planned for employee satisfaction improvement. He's going to be looking at ways to implement some of them company wide, so keep an eye out for that." Tyler rose, collecting the folders that he hadn't touched. Had he brought them just for show? Maybe they were his work, and he hadn't had time to go back to his office. "Unless there are questions, that's all I have. No? All right, get to work. The rubric should be in your email by COB."

Stephanie watched him leave the room and frowned. Something was off with him. It wasn't as if she knew him well enough to ask him to open up to her. On the other hand . . . She stood and slipped from the room while everyone else swarmed the cookie table.

She caught up with him at the elevators. "Tyler?"

He turned, finger still on the Up button. "Yeah?"

"Are you all right?"

He managed a sad smile. "Not really, but it's not work."

"Do you want to talk about it? I know we're not pals, but sometimes an unbiased ear is a good thing." She hunched her shoulders. Why was she offering?

He studied her a moment, before shaking his head. "You're not what people say you are, are you?"

"I hope not."

This time, his smile was broad and reached his eyes. "You're not alone in feeling that way, you know?"

The elevator arrived and Tyler started to step in.

Stephanie followed.

He lifted his eyebrows.

"I'm not following you, promise. I made up my mind just before the meeting that I needed to talk to Joe. I figured I'd go talk to his admin and see when he could work me in."

"Maybe I should be asking if *you're* all right."

She shook her head. "No. But I will be."

"We're not losing you, are we?"

Stephanie didn't want to answer. She didn't want to lie, but she also didn't want to admit the truth.

The elevator reached their floor and the doors slid open, saving her from responding. "I hope things work out for you, Tyler."

"Thanks. For you, too." Tyler tapped his forehead as he headed down the hall in the opposite direction.

Stephanie kept herself from shuddering—why did people insist on goofing around with salutes like that?—and aimed for Joe's admin.

"Can I help you?"

"Hi. I was wondering if there was some time this week that I could get five minutes with Joe."

"Just five?" The admin narrowed her eyes.

"Promise. It's really quick."

With a nod, the admin turned to the computer and clicked her mouse several times before looking up. "He has fifteen right now if you want."

Now? That had been her hope, sort of. But she'd also been banking on it taking a few days. She took a breath and smiled. "Sure. Thanks."

"Go ahead." The admin waved toward Joe's door.

You can do this. Just do it. Stephanie tapped on the door before pushing it open and poking her head in. "Joe?"

He glanced up from his computer and took off his glasses. "Stephanie? Come on in. Did we have an appointment?"

"No. But she said you were free. I won't take long." She scooted in the door and closed it behind herself.

His eyebrows lifted. "Uh-oh."

"No. I don't think it's that." She stood in the middle of the room at attention. It wasn't a conscious decision, but it felt right. "I wanted to let you know I'm going to be sending in my resignation this afternoon. I'd be happy to work out two weeks' notice, but I'll understand if you prefer I just go. Christopher is a great leader and will do fine taking over government services. And I think, all things considered, it's better to get out of his way."

Joe shook his head. "Sit down."

"Sir, I really—"

"Sit." He pointed to the chair in front of his desk.

Stephanie fought a sigh as she moved to the chair. She sat, back ramrod straight.

"Is this because you and Christopher broke up?"

"We were barely together."

"That doesn't answer my question."

She shrugged. "I guess. Yes. It's just hard."

"Is he treating you poorly?"

"No. He's great. He's been nothing but professional. It's me. Just like it's always me, okay? People don't like me, and that's fine. I'm intimidating and no-nonsense and I tend to blurt out what I think without pausing to phrase it more politely. So I get it. I'm working on it, but the reality is, I've ruined my reputation here, and now this thing with Chris . . . I'm better off. I think we're all better off, if I go."

Joe tented his fingers and tapped them on his chin. "Have you told Christopher?"

"No. I figured I'd wait and tell him on my last day." Or maybe never. That was also an option still in play. Definitely the most tempting option of the ones on the table.

"Tell you what. If, after you tell Christopher what you just told me, you still want to resign, I'll accept. I think this is a mistake. Not just for the company—because you're selling yourself short—but also personally. Do you still have feelings for him?"

A tear slipped down her burning cheek and she looked away. "Yes."

"Then you need to tell him that, too."

She swiped at the tears and shook her head, lurching to her feet. "He won't let me."

"Don't give him a choice."

Joe might have kept talking, but Stephanie didn't hear. She fled from his office, turning sharply to use the stairs to reduce the number of people who had to see her humiliation. She couldn't go home—all her things were still in her office—but she could take a walk. That, at least, would give her time to get her emotions under control again.

She needed to be in control when she saw Christopher.

The last thing she wanted was for him to feel sorry for her and change his reaction.

Stephanie brushed past the health nuts climbing up with a murmured, "Excuse me."

She had to get outside before anyone else saw her tears.

"I'm TELLING YOU, it was Stephanie and she was sobbing." Jess shook her head and stabbed forcefully into her salad. "You should call her."

Christopher snorted. "Stephanie does not want me to call her."

"You're pathetic." Jess dropped her fork and pushed away from the table before she stalked into the kitchen.

Christopher looked at Ryan. "What did I do? I didn't make her cry."

"Bro. Do you care about her or not?"

"It doesn't matter whether or not I care about her. She doesn't want anything to do with me." He studied the food on his plate, appetite gone. Why was she crying? She'd hurried out of the meeting on Tyler's heels. Had he said something to her? Done something? Even as his fists clenched, he worked to take a breath. It wasn't his problem. She'd told him that.

He was going to have to get over it.

"There's such a thing as being too nice. You know that, right?" Ryan pinned Christopher with a pointed look.

"No. I don't. And honestly, a guy could get whiplash. Men are supposed to respect a woman's decision, right?" Christopher pointed a finger at him. "Unless we're not, and we're supposed to fight for her. But how do you tell the difference? She was crystal clear that she wasn't going to continue to pursue a relationship with me."

"So set the relationship thing aside." Ryan batted at Christopher's pointing finger. "Aren't you friends with her?"

Christopher puffed up his cheeks and let the air pop out. "I don't know. I guess. Sort of."

"Shouldn't even sort of friends care when their sort of friend is upset enough to cry at work? Especially when that's completely out of character for said friend?" Ryan's eyebrows lifted as he glared at Christopher, driving home his point.

"Fine." Christopher sighed. "I'll talk to her tomorrow."

Jess stopped in the doorway of the kitchen. "Tomorrow? No. Get in your car and go to her house and make sure she's all right. Do it now."

"Jess. She doesn't want me at her house." That much he

knew with absolute certainty. That was her inner sanctum. She'd let him in once, and it had gone horribly, horribly wrong. She wasn't going to let him in again.

"Then she won't let you in. But what if she does?" Jess's hands hit her hips, and she glowered at him. "Don't let your pride keep you from the best thing that ever happened to you."

"She's not wrong, man. It's a lesson I had to learn myself." Ryan's gaze flicked over to Jess.

Christopher frowned. Something in the way his best friend was looking at his baby sister didn't sit right. "What about Bible study? The guys'll be here soon and I'm not sure—"

"Go. I'll get your shoes. Ry, you find his keys. You can lead the Bible study, right?" Jess jogged down the hallway toward Christopher's bedroom.

"What's going on with you and Jess?" Christopher took the keys Ryan handed him.

Ryan stiffened. "Nothing, man. We're working on the contest together, remember? You're really gone over this girl, aren't you?"

"Woman. And you're changing the subject."

"Because there's no conversation to be had on any other subject." Ryan threw his hands in the air. "Come on, man. How long have you known me?"

"Feels like it might be too long, given how bossy you've become."

Ryan laughed. "You're just trying to get out of going. She needs you, and Bible study will be fine this one time without you."

Jess came back into the room and dropped a pair of shoes at Christopher's feet. "Here. Although, maybe you should change. Those jeans are kind of ratty."

"I'm not changing so I can drive across town and not get let into someone's house." Christopher shoved his feet into his shoes. "That's a hard line in the sand right there. Don't push."

Jess held up her hands. "Okay. Geez. Try to help a guy up his game and get kicked for the effort."

"Up my game," Christopher muttered as he stood. He glared at Ryan then his sister. "I just want to go on record that this is probably the dumbest thing I've ever let you two talk me into. And that *includes* trying to climb up the outside of the band room in high school."

Ryan snickered. "That was epic. We would've made it if that lady hadn't seen us and called the cops."

"Yeah, well, she did see us, and she did call the cops." He scowled at his friend, then turned it on his sister. "And you were too busy flirting with the guy at the gas station across the street to do a decent job as lookout."

"Hey, Mom and Dad chewed me up for that, too."

"I'm just saying. This is going to be worse, and the two of you won't be around to share in the butt kicking." Maybe he wouldn't go. Maybe he'd just get in his car and drive around for an hour, then come back and say she wouldn't let him in. Except that would be lying. And knowing Jess, she'd check up on him somehow. Ugh.

"Try to keep that positive attitude. It's so endearing." Jess leaned up on her tiptoes and kissed his cheek.

"Yeah, yeah. I'll be back soon." He stomped to the door, pausing to grab his coat and shrug it on. It might be March, but the nights were still chilly.

This was such a dumb idea.

Of course, he didn't like that she'd been crying, but that wasn't his business anymore.

No matter how much he wished it was.

Christopher parked in front of Stephanie's neighbor's house. No point in advertising his presence too soon. Maybe the element of surprise would get her to open the door.

What was he doing?

He banged his head against the headrest.

Why did he let his sister and her romantic streak talk him into stuff like this? There was no backing out now.

He swallowed and pushed open the car door. Might as well go get it over with. If he hurried, he could make it back for the tail end of Bible study, since it started later this week and they weren't sharing a meal first. Which was a whole other thing to try to figure out. He liked having dinner with the guys—that was sometimes the best fellowship time. There was conversation and sharing and it wasn't awkward and weird, because they had food.

Huh. Maybe missing out on Bible study this week wasn't as awful as he'd thought.

Zipping his coat, he went around his car to the sidewalk. It wasn't super cold out, but he still kept a brisk pace as he walked to Stephanie's driveway. He took a deep breath and went up, over the flagstone path, to her front door. He pushed the doorbell.

The chimes echoed through the house.

He tucked his hands in his pockets and waited. She would see him on the porch through the sidelights as soon as she got to her foyer. Would she turn around and walk back away?

Or was she going to ignore the doorbell altogether? Her Jeep was in the carport, so she had to be home. Didn't she?

Stephanie stepped into the foyer, her pace slowing as she spotted him. She stopped. Frowned.

Christopher lifted a hand in a half-hearted wave, one corner of his mouth twisted into a smile.

She stood there what felt like a full minute before shaking her head and walking to the door. She opened it a crack. "What do you want?"

"Can I come in and talk to you?"

"There's nothing to say."

"I think there is. Look, Jess saw you crying in the stairwell today. She mentioned it to me, and I'm worried about you. Are you okay?" Should he add that Jess was worried, too? No. Why would Stephanie care about that?

Stephanie sighed and widened the opening. "I'm fine. Come on in. I was going to talk to you at the office tomorrow, but since you're here, we might as well do it now."

He frowned as he stepped into the house. What did that mean?

"Come on through to the living room." Stephanie shut the door and started in that direction. She was wearing a tank top and stretchy leggings. A faint sheen of sweat covered her skin.

She looked amazing.

He'd known she was fit, but she didn't dress to show off her curves. Workout gear left nothing to the imagination.

It also put the scars that covered her left arm on display. That must have hurt. She'd mentioned her injury—the one that had ended her Army career—but she'd downplayed the severity.

It just made her more beautiful.

He swallowed. *Not the point, man. Not even remotely the point. Focus.*

"You can sit there." She pointed to an arm chair, then perched on the edge of the coffee table in the middle of the room.

With a shrug, he sat where she'd indicated. "What's up?"

"I talked to Joe this afternoon—after the meeting with Tyler. I wanted to let him know in person that I was resigning."

Christopher blinked. Resigning? "From the contest? Don't do that. You're more qualified than I am, and I know he sees it. At this point, my goal is to do whatever it takes to make sure they see how much they need to give the position to you."

She shook her head, her eyes glistening. "Not just the contest. From the company. I've already had a couple of calls from recruiters since I activated my résumé. I'm going to be fine. And I think the company is better off without me."

"What? No. It's not. Look, if being around me is that awful, let me leave. I'm sorry. I never wanted to make you feel this uncomfortable." His heart was in his stomach, and that was sinking into his shoes. She couldn't leave.

"That's not true. You know my reputation."

"You're right, I do. People say you're talented. A leader. Motivated and able to keep contracts on time and on budget. You're good at your job, Stephanie. That's not a bad thing."

"That's not what people say. They use the 'b' word a lot."

He closed his eyes and shot up a quick prayer for the right words. He opened his eyes and scooted forward so their knees bumped. Christopher moved his head until their gazes met.

"Anyone who uses that word—or anything else that's pejorative when they're talking about you—is a small-minded fool. I get that it hurts. I do. But don't let them win. Especially not when they're wrong."

She frowned, her eyebrows drawing together. "But you—"

"I was wrong. And I didn't know what I was talking about. And I will admit to being a little jealous and also intimidated. None of which has anything to do with you. It was all me. And it's all changed. I don't see that anymore. And I look back and I wonder how I convinced myself I ever saw it in the first place. You're amazing. The company needs you." He paused and took a deep breath. He could stop there. It might save his ego, but it wouldn't be the full truth. She deserved the whole story. "I need you."

Stephanie stiffened. "I don't understand."

He laughed and scrubbed his hands over his face. "Of course, you don't. I don't want you to go. It's not all just about the company. I personally don't want you to go—I want you to stay, and I want us to keep working together, and I'm begging you to forgive me and give me a second chance. I promise I won't screw it up this time."

Her tongue darted between her lips. "I thought you hated me."

"Quite the opposite."

Stephanie's lips twitched. "Did you just quote Jane Austen?"

"I have a sister, what can I say?" He grinned and leaned forward to take her hand. He rested his forehead on hers. "Jess told me I needed to fight for you—I convinced myself you wouldn't want that."

"Every woman wants a man who's going to fight for her."

He laughed. "Score one for Jess."

"Did she tell you what to do after you won?"

Christopher looked into her eyes and lost himself. He inched forward. "I think I can figure that out for myself."

He lowered his mouth to hers. The time for overthinking was definitely at an end.

∼

"You ready?"

Stephanie looked around her computer monitor and grinned. Her heart leapt—still—to see Christopher waiting for her. It'd been two months, almost to the day, actually, since he came to her house to see what was wrong. Those months had been glorious.

That wasn't to say they didn't bicker. They did. But under it was a stronger foundation than they'd had previously, so disagreements didn't do more than ruffle the waters.

And keep things lively.

She stood, crossed to him, leaned up and kissed his cheek, pausing to whisper in his ear, "I love you."

"I love you, too." He brushed his lips over hers then tugged her hand. "Come on. I'm hungry."

She laughed. "Did you skip lunch again?"

"Not on purpose. Meeting ran long. But I think we have a strong proposal and the client is going to appreciate our attention to detail."

"That's what I love to hear." She grinned and hurried back to her desk to shut down her laptop and pack up for the day. New business was steadily increasing. She and Christopher made a good team—something Joe had figured out before they did, apparently. "I saw a new request for a proposal this morning that I put Danica and Zoe on."

"Yeah? They're a good team—if it's a fit, they'll figure out how." He laced his fingers through hers.

"That's what I thought. I'm glad Danica decided to stay once Rick was gone. She's an asset we need." Stephanie flicked off the light and closed her office door. They chatted about work on the way to the car. She'd started picking Christopher up on her way in to work most days. It made hanging out together afterward easier—and that was something they both appreciated. "When are you going to tell me where we're eating?"

He grinned. "When we get there."

She shook her head. He had something up his sleeve. He'd been awfully sneaky about this dinner. "Is it to celebrate having only two months left in the contest?"

He shook his head.

She clicked the fob to unlock the Jeep and tossed her bags in the back. As she climbed in behind the wheel, Christopher settled in the passenger seat. "To celebrate two months officially together?"

"Warmer." He chuckled. "Are you going to keep asking?"

"I don't love surprises. I thought you knew this."

He frowned. "You really want to know?"

"I really do."

"All right, but just remember, you forced my hand."

She lifted her eyebrows as he popped open the glove compartment. What on earth was in there?

"This isn't my plan. Again, just so you're clear."

"Got it. I ruined it, just tell me." She laughed.

Christopher pulled out a small black box and flipped it open as he shifted in his seat. "Will you marry me?"

A trio of diamonds winked atop a gold band. Her heart stopped, then took off at a gallop. They'd talked about marriage a few times—in what she'd thought was a more hypothetical conversation than he had, apparently. Stephanie tore her eyes away from the ring and up to Christopher. "Oh, wow. Yes!"

She thrust out her left hand, laughing as he slipped the ring on her finger. "This probably would have been better at a restaurant, but you have to admit, doing it this way is more us."

He leaned across the console to kiss her. "I guess it is. I love you. Even if you spoil my surprises."

"I love you too." There might be two more months left in Joe Robinson's contest, but Stephanie had officially already won the prize.

EPILOGUE

Five *months ago, at the company Christmas party*

Jessica Ward shook her head. *Dumbest move ever.* Why would Joe Robinson decide to break up the company? Not that it probably mattered to her. She wasn't very high on the totem pole. And she liked it that way.

Keeping a low profile meant no one was paying a whole lot of attention. And that meant she could still dabble here and there to keep her hacking skills honed. She didn't do any damage—she wasn't a thief—she just loved puzzles that came with a bit of adrenaline.

She glanced over at Ryan Foster. He was talking, arms waving wildly, with her brother Christopher. The two of them had been best friends since forever. And he didn't notice her either, except as Chris's annoying little sister.

Sometimes staying under the radar was a serious pain in the rear.

She glanced down at the form-fitting, sparkly cocktail dress she'd splurged on for the Christmas party. She'd gotten appreciative looks from a couple of the guys she worked with, but most of them had brought dates.

Anyway, it wasn't as if she cared about what any of them thought.

She looked over at Ryan again and sighed. What was it going to take to get him to notice her? And if he did, would her brother let him live? No. One problem at a time.

Step one: get Ryan to look her way and actually *see* her.

Worry about Christopher after that.

Jess stood and crossed to the table where Ryan and Chris were parked. "I'm bored."

"Seriously?" Ryan shook his head. "How? It's a party."

"Everyone's dancing but me." She tried for a pout—it was a little underhanded and more girly than she usually bothered with, but apparently it worked.

"Why don't you take her for a spin, Ry? I'm going to hit the dessert table." Christopher socked Ryan on the arm as he stood. "You look nice, Jess."

"Thanks." She caught Ryan nodding, and her cheeks warmed. Maybe the dress hadn't been a complete waste of money.

"Come on, pipsqueak. If we're gonna dance, let's dance." Ryan offered his hand and led her out onto the dance floor.

The song was slow, so she stepped into his arms. His hand was warm and firm at her waist.

This was exactly where she wanted to be.

If only she could convince Ryan that he wanted it, too.

READ about Jess and Ryan in So You Love Your Best Friend's Sister.

ACKNOWLEDGMENTS

Thank you for reading *So You Love to Hate Your Boss*! This is book 2 in my new So You Want to Be a Billionaire series. Book 1 (*So You Want a Second Chance*) was part of the Love's Treasure Collection pre-order bonuses prior to publication. The remaining 4 books in the series will be released, one each month, starting with book 3, *So You Love Your Best Friend's Sister*, in July 2021. All of the books will be available in Kindle Unlimited and for purchase on Amazon. I hope you enjoy the rest of my little twist on billionaires!

You can find all my books and sign up for my monthly(ish) newsletter on my website: www.ElizabethMaddrey.com

Thanks as always to my family for encouraging me in my writing endeavors - be that through space and time or for simply telling me they're proud of me. I couldn't do it without you.

Thanks also to writing friends - particularly Valerie Comer and the gals in the writing squad.

Finally, none of this would work if I didn't have inspiration, and that comes only from my Heavenly Father.

WANT A FREE BOOK?

If you enjoyed this book and would like to read another of my books for free, you can get a free e-book simply by signing up for my newsletter on my website.

OTHER BOOKS BY ELIZABETH MADDREY

So You Want to Be a Billionaire

So You Want a Second Chance

So You Love to Hate Your Boss

So You Love Your Best Friend's Sister

So You Have My Secret Baby

So You Need a Fake Relationship

So You Forgot You Love Me

Hope Ranch Series

So You Love Your Best Friend's Sister

Hope for Tomorrow

Hope for Love

Hope for Freedom

Hope for Family

Hope at Last

Peacock Hill Romance Series

A Heart Restored

A Heart Reclaimed

A Heart Realigned

A Heart Redirected

A Heart Rearranged

A Heart Reconsidered

Arcadia Valley Romance – Baxter Family Bakery Series

Loaves & Wishes

Muffins & Moonbeams

Cookies & Candlelight

Donuts & Daydreams

The 'Operation Romance' Series

Operation Mistletoe

Operation Valentine

Operation Fireworks

Operation Back-to-School

Prefer to read a box set? Find the whole series here.

The 'Taste of Romance' Series

A Splash of Substance

A Pinch of Promise

A Dash of Daring

A Handful of Hope

A Tidbit of Trust

Prefer to read a box set? Get the series in two parts! Box 1 and Box 2.

The 'Grant Us Grace' Series

Wisdom to Know

Courage to Change

Serenity to Accept

Joint Venture

Pathway to Peace

Prefer to read a box set? Grab the whole series here.

The 'Remnants' Series:

Faith Departed

Hope Deferred

Love Defined

Stand alone novellas

Kinsale Kisses: An Irish Romance

Luna Rosa (part of A Tuscan Legacy)

Non-Fiction

A Walk in the Valley: Christian encouragement for your journey
through infertility

For the most recent listing of all my books, please visit my website.

ABOUT THE AUTHOR

Elizabeth Maddrey is a semi-reformed computer geek and homeschooling mother of two who lives in the suburbs of Washington D.C. When she isn't writing, Elizabeth is a voracious consumer of books. She loves to write about Christians who struggle through their lives, dealing with sin and receiving God's grace on their way to their own romantic happily ever after.

- facebook.com/ElizabethMaddrey
- instagram.com/ElizabethMaddrey
- amazon.com/Elizabeth-Maddrey/e/B00A11QGME
- bookbub.com/authors/elizabeth-maddrey